Table of Contents

Text copyright © 2021 by Henry Sipes

ISBN: 9798505319833

Independently Published

Cover Art Credit: Pixabay, Planets from KELLEPICS and Angel from Comfreak

Preface

The idea for this novel began back in 2015 after the death of my first wife. Having just finished my master's degree in astronomy from Swinburne University, the game plan was to start teaching part time. Best laid plans as they say. I wanted to use what I had learned before it slowly dripped away. One of my class projects was an orbital platform for science and tourism. The craft used some of the best real spacecraft elements of the day and research on environmental control systems and propulsion systems that were and are essentially "green". Some of these sadly have stagnated over the years being shelved and mothballed through various US administrations. My idea was shelved itself for a while as God had other plans.

My younger brother was probably one of the smartest people I will ever know. Boy could he make me mad though. I remember arguing with him on the long bus ride home from high school as we rode across the farmland of Meade County, KY. One day, he looks at me knowing he was going to goad me into an argument and says, "You are eating pig shit." I say, "I am not" and of course he would reply, "Yes you are." The fight was on. Though I was correct, so was he. No, we did not really have pig shit in our mouths, but as he stated, "If you can smell it, it is in your lungs. If you open your mouth, it is in your mouth." I look at him all frustrated and said, "What in the hell are you talking about, Mark?" "Methane, it is part of pig shit and you are breathing it and swallowing it right now!" He had me. At the molecular level, he was right. We were taking in some small portion of pig shit in our mouths. Neither of us was wrong if we could just listen to the other's point of view.

Lillian Banks, God rest his soul, was pestering me one day on that same school bus. He would sit behind me tickling and flicking my ears. He was trying to get a rise out of me. One day he finally did, and I turned around having my fill and said words that still make me sad to this day. I said, "Stop it, Boy!" I understood *Boy* was not a word to call a young black man, but I was tired of being picked on and I knew that word would sting. I knew it would hurt. Lillian could have knocked my block off that day which would have gotten him in trouble, perhaps suspended. Instead, lightning fast, he slapped me across the right cheek when the bus driver was not looking, scolding me, "You do not call me boy!" Following the teaching of Jesus, I turned the other cheek and called him "Boy!" again and of course he slapped that cheek as well. My face burned long after I climbed down the stairs of the bus. The guilt of using that word burned my soul even longer. Did I really understand what it was like to be a young black man? Did I truly understand Lillian's point of view?

There was a time I believed as a child in the faith of my family. Losing my brother made me question that faith. Questioning that faith made me listen and observe what was happening around me. When my fellow Christians condemned a man running for president for the color of his skin, I questioned. When the leaders of my religion, one canonized as a saint, knowingly promoted those guilty of sexual assault, I questioned. When those I was raised to respect, the elders of my Church, condemned Muslims for the garments they wore to praise God, I questioned. Strange how it was acceptable for Catholics that loved God to wear coverings, but we judge Muslims who also love God for doing the same. When my fellow Christians supported a candidate who openly degraded women and Hispanics, I questioned. Is a white Christian male an oxymoron? I questioned, but I stayed silent. I can stay silent no more.

At heart, I am a futurist and an eternal optimist. At the time of this writing, SpaceX has finally nailed the landing of the SN15 Starship prototype. The possibilities are endless for humanity if we open our hearts and our minds and listen to the point of view of each other. What if we come together as the true descendants of Abraham and join hand in hand, passing not judgment upon our brothers and sisters, but loving our neighbors no matter their color, religion, or beliefs? What if we delight in our diversity? I believe if we can do these things and more, we can avoid the reckoning coming. The best of humanity can move forward beyond our world.

This is a story of hope and damnation. This is a story about faith. Let us pray that we can accept another point of view. We are otherwise lost.

Acknowledgements

This has been a work of love and a work of faith. Without the support of many, it would not have been possible. Frankly, without the Covid-19 Pandemic, the time may not have been available. I had to go to some dark places forgotten from days gone by. I even shed a few tears praying and writing to hopefully achieve balance. Without the love and support of my wonderful wife, Tonya, this work would not have been possible.

I want to also thank others in my life that have supported me along the way or contributed in some fashion to this work. I must thank my sister, Mary, for being the first rebel. I must thank my younger brother, Mark Leo, for being a real pain in the ass. He left this world far too soon. To my older brother Louis, who taught me not to believe everything that was written or spoken and only half of what was seen. I thank you. I must give thanks and respect to my parents, Ann and Joe, for understanding my faith is not their faith. I would be remiss if I did not thank Lillian for not knocking my block off that day. Thank you for smiling as you made me understand what it meant to turn the other cheek.

We all have someone in our lives that gave us a nudge in the right direction along the way. At the time it seemed insignificant, but our librarian at Flaherty Elementary and Middle School made such a contribution. Sister Carolita could read my soul. One day, she pulls off the shelf a copy of C.S. Lewis's *The Lion, the Witch, and the Wardrobe*. From that day forward, I have never stopped reading science fiction and fantasy. God bless you Sister Carolita.

Special thanks should go out to Gabor Bihari, Department of Experimental Physics, University of Debrecen, Hungary, for sharing his research on thorium drives with me.

Thanks to the many editors of this work; Ann, Joe, Pat, Tonya, and others. Any errors found within are still my responsibility. To Mohamed J. Alani for checking my Arabic translations, I wish you all the best in Iraq. Stay safe my friend and you are always welcome to visit us again in Kentucky.

I love you all, every single one. May the hand of the one true God be upon you all. Yad Allah ealayk!

Prologue

In the year of our Lord 2344

"Papi, Papi, please tell us the story, please!!!" Jennifer called out.

"Ok, I guess I can tell you the story. After all, this is our 12,000th *Pay the Dirt* ceremony on Al-Ruh. Let me see, how should I begin?" As I thought out loud, this was a story for all, but not necessarily a story for the youngsters in this motley group of Sister Anna's 2nd graders. There were many dark days for our crew and passengers of NUERA1. To tell this story and not scare the little ones, I had better leave out the worst. But as Bishop Rogers always said, it is important that they all understand the light and the dark.

"Ok, ok, but first, a prayer. In the name of the Father, the Son, and the Holy Spirit. Blessed Father, protect these youth as they face the everyday trials of life on Al-Ruh. Help them follow the teachings of Sister Anna. Guide them into the light and forever protect them from the dark. In Your name, I pray." As I blessed the 2nd graders, I remembered the first priest of NUERA1, Father Joe, and what he must have faced on that initial voyage. How he must have been filled with doubts, but then the freedoms our blessed Pope Vieira must have given young Father Joe were boundless, almost.

"We cannot speak of NUERA1 and the launch without starting at the very beginning. Does anyone remember their names?" I asked knowing full well that they all knew the names by heart. All members of the congregation of Gliese knew the entire tree. As the memorial at Landing Springs, had every name engraved on each leaf of the stone tree; all one hundred names of the original NUERA1 crew and compliment. It was our only link to the past or so most Gliesiens thought. As a priest, I knew there was something else hidden in the chapel, where a small group of clergy, sworn to secrecy, kept the artifact. "Children, our story begins in 2014 with the covenant, though perhaps I should start in the true beginning...let me see, that was about 2009."

Chapter 1

In the year of our Lord 2009

"Holy Father, you must rest. Tomorrow is a great day of celebration, your celebration, your birthday," spoke Monsignor Mike to his Holiness Pope Bessarion. Monsignor Mike had worked for his Holiness since the beginning of his time as Pope, the leader of the Catholic Church. Among his many duties, was serving his Holiness communion, attending to his nightly prayers, and he was among only a few who knew the true sufferings of his Holiness.

"My true friend, Mickey, you know my dreams of late have been restless. I feel that I suffer for my sins during my last days of serving our Lord. I will go to bed now my friend. Pray for me to suffer no more and sleep for eternity." Monsignor Mike prayed the Lord's

Prayer with Pope Bessarion and left him to his privacy
in his holy chambers.

"Lord, I am but your humble servant, I am a
hypocrite and a sinner. Forgive me my sins and the sins
of my followers, and let me rest for once this night."
Pope Bessarion spoke these words as he rolled into bed,
but not believing he would rest any better than the last
days of this month. "Father stop, Father stop, Father
stop, forgive me Father, but please stop," yelled little
Jake as he tore from the pews of the Church darkened
with the sins of Father Bessarion.

Pope Bessarion woke with a jolt sitting upright in a
pool of cold sweat surrounded by darkness. Then from
out of the darkness, the light burst forth in blinding
wonder with unbearable heat burning his soul. "Father
Bessarion, you are not worthy to receive the title of
Pope. You are not worthy to speak even the words of
the Our Father," a voice hissed through the light. "But
God says we are but servants to Him, and must do His

bidding until the final days. I speak your burden, Father Bessarion. I speak your only path to forgiveness."

Pope Bessarion spoke with reverence and kneeled to the light and said, "I will do anything you ask, just make the pain stop. You are burning my flesh. I cannot bear the light. I cannot bear the pain."

"YOU WILL BEAR THE PAIN OF THOSE YOU HAVE SINNED AGAINST FATHER BESSARION. YOU HAVE FORSAKEN THE LIGHT FOR THE SINS OF THE FLESH." The light faded a fraction as another voice spoke, "Gabriel, enough, now speak his forgiveness as he is human." The Voice spoke and Gabriel obeyed.

"The wealth you have hoarded shall be returned to the light and to the humble and the meek. Send forth your servant, Mickey, and the Order to collect all the gold from every Church, chapel, chalice, cross, and spoon in every Catholic corner of the world. Tell no one the purpose. Disguise the truth with false gold instead until your replacement comes to free you. One follows after you. Do not accept his resignation as he will replace your wretched soul as a true follower of Christ. Mario Santos comes to save your flock from eternal fire. Mario's resignation attempt will be the time to act. The next conclave will select him as pope. You must convince him to take the papal name of António Vieira. Speak of this to no one but your servant, Mickey, as his soul is pure and his life protected by my brothers and sisters for a time."

"Your Holiness," pleaded Monsignor Mike, "Your Holiness you must awaken," shook Monsignor Mike of the Pope's bed.

Pope Bessarion, startled awake by the sounds of Monsignor Mike, still sweating from his nightmares, called Monsignor Mike close. "Mickey, my most trusted friend and warrior of the truth, the way, a true believer in Jesus Christ, I have a most unhealthy task for you. Your life belongs to Christ and as I am the living representative of Christ on Earth, I give you this trial. Go forth, Mickey, and collect what has possessed the souls of our followers since time immortal. Go forth, Mickey, and bring that which has possessed the Church and nearly destroyed us. Bring the gold of Christ back to the fold. May God have mercy on you. Trust no one in this endeavor but the Militia Sancti Petri. As God has spoken, every last drop of gold must return to the Vatican in two years time. Be not afraid my friend. The angel Gabriel himself will protect you as well as the Militia Sancti Petri."

August, in the year of our Lord 2011
Vatican City, Rome

The hot August nights of summer had not escaped the Vatican. Monsignor Mike Flaherty felt as old as the sun itself as he crossed the courtyard to pay his respects to Pope Bessarion. Looking over his shoulder he could faintly see the shadows of his ever vigilant guard, Archangel Gabriel. He grasped for the cross beneath his tunic and held tightly as he prayed for forgiveness for what he deemed were sins against everything he believed. He had killed not once but several times over the last couple of years. He told himself it was for the good of the Church and for the Pope's vision. But God said not to kill. True, he would now be dead with his head on a platter, if he had not fought for his life. The sword of Gabriel was dark black with the blood of hundreds that had tried to take from them what was the gold of Christ. The Monsignor had seen many things unseen for thousands of years; dark things rising up in human form upon the Earth.

"Your Holiness, my most holy Pope Bessarion, I have returned," spoke Mickey as he entered the private chambers of Pope Bessarion. Mickey almost stumbled to the stone floor as he fought for composure after seeing the sunken pale white face of his Holiness. These past years had not been good to his master.

"Ah, my faithful servant, Mickey, it is good to see you, my friend. May His hand be upon you for your service to our cause," Pope Bessarion coughed hard into his handkerchief with scarlet red shining through. "Now bow before me and let me absolve you of your sins." Pope Bessarion received Mickey's confession.

"Mickey, the vaults below are teeming to the rim with His gold. You have achieved that which I did not believe possible in only two years. Now you can rest but not within these walls. There is but one task left that He requests from you. In one month's time, on His most holy day of rest, the fourth of September, you must have all the gold melted down into bars in preparation to be sold. Everything has been prepared for your retirement in America. An account has been setup for the Vatican that only our future Pope can access. Sell all of the gold on the sixth of September and have all

the money wired to this account, 6669996669992025,"
said Pope Bessarion as he coughed so hard Mickey
thought he would pass out from exhaustion.

"Your Holiness, please sit down and let me help
you." Mickey thought the end of days were upon the
Earth as he memorized the account number and then
burned the piece of paper upon which it was written.
"My friend Mickey, there is one little side trip I need
you to make to South America," his Holiness pressed
upon Mickey. "You must go to visit Mario and press
him into service again for our Lord. You must go at
once and then you can retire to America. Remember
Mickey, you must forget your former life." As Mickey
left to go to the private helipad of the Pope, Mickey
thought he would never forget the blood upon his hands
until he was called again.

September 6th

Gold prices had taken a short but significant dip as the market opened. Throughout the month of September in 2011, gold continued to drop in price with no one the wiser or with the understanding that this was the end of the last bull gold market in the history of the world. An offshore Swiss account, 6669996669992025, in the name of the then unknown, Mario Santos, grew in size in the billions. An AI super computer deep in a vault in Washington D.C. silently recorded the event flagged for later review.

In the year of our Lord 2012
In the mountains near Safford, Arizona

Mary Harrington had been awake almost 24 hours straight watching the data streaming across the flat screen monitor of the Vatican's imaging system for the

Vatican Advanced Technology Telescope (VATT). She was following up on data originally taken by the High Accuracy Radial velocity Planet Searcher (HARPS) at the European Southern Observatory in Chile. The HARPS spectrograph compares the spectrum of a star simultaneously with the spectrum from a thorium lamp and can detect the minute gravitational pull of a planet as it orbits its central star. The effects of several cups of coffee were starting to fade as Mary began to nod off to sleep. She kept trying to hum a song she sang to her daughter when trying to explain the gravitational wobble of a star. "Weebles wobble, but they don't fall down, because the gravity of one pulls the other around." Mary sang to herself as she tried to watch the data looking for the ever so slight dip in the light output coming from the star Gliese 667C. Mary had spent every free night away from the university trying to record transits of the planets discovered by the HARPS instrument. As Mary finally lost her battle to sleep, the light curve she was capturing began to repeat signaling a periodic change.

Mary jerked as something awoke her from her slumber. Something tickled her leg and she jumped thinking it was one of those pesky observatory spiders. Then she realized it was cold coffee dripping from the cup she had overturned as she nodded off to sleep. Her computer monitor had a flashing red icon which had tried to alert the user, Mary in this case, that it had found a periodic reduction in light from Gliese 667C. She gasped as she realized the data was real. There were at least six planets circling the star as she had confirmed the HARPS data. No, it cannot be! Mary thought as she looked closer at the data. The data also confirmed that three of the planets were in the *Goldilock's zone* of habitability. Everyone had been concentrating on the HARPS data for the small exoplanet, Gliese667C (c). As her colleagues reminded, it would probably be tidally locked at its distance from the central star. Here now she had confirmed with an entirely different method for planet detection, transit, that there were three planets in the habitable zone; besides Gliese667C (c), there was a (d), and an (e). Something kept bugging Mary in the back of her mind about there being three. She could not remember which Sister. When she was young, one of the Sisters at St. Patrick's was trying to impress the class about the Holy Trinity, the Father, the Son, and the Holy Spirit. Oh, my mind is wondering now and grasping for truths not seen. Time to close up for the night and get some much needed sleep, she thought. Several thousand miles away in Castel Gandolfo near Rome, the home of the Vatican's other observatory, computers were recording the same signals backing up the data.

In the year of our Lord 2014

Somewhere over Syria

Jake's FB-22 Raptor had seen clear skies and smooth air for the past hour flying at Mach 2.5. The publicly stated speed was Mach 1.8 but the Raptor still had a few secrets left. Warning alarms started going off as he entered Syrian air space and the automatic bombing pattern program initiated. Jake leaned back and took a deep breath as he hated the automation. The old days of seat of your pants flying were gone. Suddenly, a rather loud wailing alarm sounded and the computer paused...."Pilot, do you wish to abort the run...SAMs are tracking us....probability of completion is 60%." Well, Jake thought, 60% is better than nothing when suddenly his aircraft banked to the right. "Pilot Young, probability of completion is 40%...tracking multiple SAMs homing in on our signal." Damn, Jake thought, nothing could home in on a Raptor, or at least that is what the instructors always said. Jake hit the abort program button and took the bull by the horns.

"Computer, spray starburst pattern of ...." "Imminent impact, imminent impact, in five, four..." Jake banked hard to the left until he almost blacked out and then pulled up hard and hit the afterburners aiming for space. Another secret that the public tax payers did not know was that the Raptor could reach altitudes of 100,000 feet with the help of some on board rockets. Jake reached and hit the button to drill a hole in the sky. One side affect was a total blackout for a few seconds as the onboard rocket system slammed Jake against the seat reaching g-forces beyond what his suit could handle. Jake woke up but something was wrong. Instead of seeing stars in front of him, all he could see were the sands of Syria growing all too fast in size. After Jake had blacked out, a specially modified SAM continued to track his Raptor and plunged right up his left engine tail pipe. Lights were flashing all over his cockpit and warning alarms were screaming at him to eject. Jake reached beneath his flight suit and pulled out his crucifix. Kissing it, he prayed and pulled the eject lever. The loud sound of the explosive bolts was still ringing in his ears, when his chute deployed and Jake floated towards the hot desert sands of Syria.

Jake could see his Raptor hit the sand in a fiery explosion below. He attempted to steer his chute away from the jet as that would mean a quick fiery death. It would also be a place guaranteed to be overrun with enemy troops within the hour searching for tech. Jake's chute was not steering correctly and he could see the problem. Several of his guide ropes had been cut during his ejection. Jake said yet another prayer and reached up with his knife to cut a few more guide ropes to straighten up his glide path. He was losing altitude fast and only just cut a rope when he had to pull hard to just miss the flames still rising from his craft as he plunged hard to the sand.

Jake gained his feet quickly as his training took over. Instead of hiding his chute to avoid detection, Jake quickly grabbed his evac kit from the ejection seat and started running away from his Raptor towards the south. He sensed he was being watched from the north as he hit the sand. ***Pop, Pop, Pop, Pop*** sand bounced all around Jake as death tried to bring him down with the lead of an AK-47. His senses had been right as an entire convoy of vehicles topped the rise to his north. Jake turned to see the ISIS rebels grinning in victory as they prepared to gun him down. ***Whoosh, whoosh, whoosh, whoosh, whoosh*** it can't be thought Jake, not out here in the deserts of Syria, but he swore he heard the sounds of a wild turkey flying from its roost. Any good for nothing Kentucky boy had heard this sound, which can only be described as the loudest thundering of wings to ever break the quiet of a damp spring morning the first day of turkey season. Jake turned to the west where the sun was just beginning to set, but all he could see was white light. Then out of the light, he could see actual wings. Wings the size of one side of his Raptor reached almost 15 feet from tip to tip. ***Thump, Thump, Thump, Thump, Thump,*** Jake could hear the sounds of an M-60 opening up from the rebel convoy. Must have taken it from my brothers, he thought. Wings or no wings, Jake thought this day was about done. The Syrians had them outnumbered 100 to 2 and those odds are not good. Jake turned to face the creature and uttered but one word, "Holy Shi...." as he could see the wings were attached to a man. An angel, thought Jake? Here in the deserts of Syria? Jake thought he must have hit his head as he ejected. The angel rose to its full height of 8 feet and with a staff in its hands, rammed the staff into the ground and boomed, "Yahweh." The very sand particles themselves vibrated to life when the word was spoken. Each particle of sand rose in sync, as a wave of sand emerged from the desert like a river. With a crack, the sand streamed forward into the Syrian convoy and shredded the very skin from the rebels until there was not a soul left but one.

The angel raised the staff and motioned over the last survivor of the convoy. The almond skinned man, wiser than the grey hairs of his head defined him, sank to his knees in front of the angel and yelled "Mikaeel, Alsalam ealaykum, Alsalam ealaykum, Alsalam ealaykum."

Jake lowered his 9mm Beretta and also sank to his knees offering, "Archangel Michael, Peace be upon you." Even as a failed Catholic, Jake knew the angels.

Archangel Michael spoke, "Rise, friends, for I am not to be kneeled to or praised. He will come that will yield the true staff of justice. You both have been called forth to serve as true believers of His word. Your contributions, Hayat, as a member of the Syrian Democratic Forces, infiltrating the ISIS heretics, and Jake, as a member of the US Air Force fighting from above to end this affront against Him, are commendable. However, it is your sufferings in His name throughout your lives that He respects the most.

Soon you will be called by the one who speaks for Him on Earth. Listen for the time when His servant will need you. Lay down your weapons, my friends, and rejoice for your path is not to death but to glory in the heavens."

As Archangel Michael vanished into the brightness of the setting desert Sun, Jake thought nobody, and especially his commanders, would believe this. Perhaps this was something best left out of the report, but how to explain his escape from the convoy? As Jake turned around the entire horizon was empty except for his fallen Raptor. The wave of destruction from Archangel Michael had not only cleaned the bones of his captors to be, but the entire convoy had been erased. The almond skinned man was no where to be found.

A small town in Kentucky

"My thoughts have made me weary these last few nights as I prepared for today's homily," spoke Father Joe as he began. The Sun was shining brilliantly through the stain glass windows onto Joe's arm warming his ebony skin as if giving him that extra bit of energy needed to speak his mind. The silence in the church that day was razored with an edge of expectation as Father Joe approached the podium. Most of the every Sunday congregation knew Father well enough that they could read his face. His expression approached painful anger, like a knife cuts deep into flesh. Father Joe had never experienced rage like this in the house of God. Yet it was God pushing him to release upon his opening line of the homily.

"Judge me, my friends, will you? Turn your back on your friends, you will. Punish the innocent, you are. Turning your back on God, you have. Forget the most important words of His Son, our Lord Jesus Christ, you have. The words of our most innocent and our most precious betray your thoughts. YOU DO NOT HAVE THE RIGHT OR THE POWER TO JUDGE. YOU ARE NOT GOD. You claim to believe in the Holy body and blood. You sign the Father, the Son, and the Holy Spirit. Blasphemy I scream at you. Did you not think that our children mimic their parents? You send them out to poke fun, to hurt, to rip the very flesh from those who do not mirror your reflection. And you come to seek my forgiveness? Did you think the souls would not sing their pain to me? Jesus was a Jew, yet you cut open the hearts of his family. He reached out to all of God's flock and you scream, 'Kill them they are Muslims.' Jesus spoke nothing about sexual orientation, but you bully them and judge with Lucifer's touch."

At this point little Mark Leo, on the front pew, began to slide further and further towards the floor scared of this new figure in church that was always so free with the candy suckers. Mark usually lost his concentration at the word go. This morning was an eye opener for him. Something was odd about Father Joe and not just his voice. Little Mark saw something for just a split second that only a few other kids noticed. Father Joe was glowing. He was not just glowing, but he had wings?? Mark thought maybe he had too many suckers before church.

The candles were flickering madly as Father Joe continued. "I, the angel of death cry for thee. I, the Son of God mourn for thee. I, the mother of Christ, gave my Son for thee. You conservative Christians call yourselves followers of Christ, yet you stop my family at your borders. You scream foul when your riches are slightly shaved for the good of all. You forget Jesus gave His very life, His last drop of blood for you and yet you cannot share? All you have is because of Me, for I gave you life. Yet, you bow down on your knees on Sunday, and forget the words my Son left for you. You sink into the darkness of the Earth, forgetting His first commandment, placing a few notes and a bit of cloth above Him."

Abor Jones reached down and picked up his son, Mark, as tears were rolling down his cheeks. He could taste the salt in his mouth trembling feeling the power of Father Joe's words. He began to weep openly as he saw the sign God was sending him. For the past few years, he had worked tirelessly developing a new type of nuclear reactor that would not yield fuel for weapons of mass destruction. Instead of the uranium that the hawks of war like Senator Buchanan had craved for years to power their submarines or to one day make them destroyers of cities, Abor had been using thorium. Ridiculed by his colleagues and almost penniless, Abornazine, keeper of the flame, and a proud member of the Abenaki indian tribe, built a thorium reactor in his basement that could power cars, houses, cities, and even spaceships.

Though a member of Father Joe's congregation, Abor still followed the ways of his tribe, his true country, the Abenaki nation. Abor had a vision from the Great Spirit that he was the keeper of the true flame, a holy flame that would not destroy but instead, preserve all true followers of the Great Spirit. His vision had told him that one day a priest would come to guide him, to lead him into the light.

"These words are not my own," Father Joe continued. "I did not prepare this sermon. The words were not written or typed. God spoke these words in my mind, as I entered the sacristy this morning. They are His hope as our Father loves us. They are His hope as His true disciples and apostles have asked for a second chance. One last chance to prove we are deserving of His forgiveness. Prepare yourselves, for some of you will be called. Prepare yourselves, because some of you are already damned. My friends, we will continue this conversation another day. Please all bow your heads to prepare and receive the Lord's blessing."

Chapter 2

22 light-years away

The planets of Abu, Ibn, and Al-Ruh had been intertwined in a dance of life for millions of years, as their star Wahid made its travels around the center of the galaxy. The close proximity of their orbits to one another around Wahid prevented each one from being tidally locked. Each relied on the other for survival around their home star. The trinity of planets harbored life that had thrived since the beginning. Tsiera looked down at the *bug* she was holding in great anticipation. She awaited the emergence of the fluorescence that would guide her through the darkness quickly approaching, as Wahid traveled down the arc to the sea. Her planet of Al-Ruh teemed with fluorescent life of all kinds. The fluorescence was a necessary adaptation due to the low light level of Wahid. Tsiera had her own adaptations to life on Al-Ruh. Her eyes were large elliptical ovals protruding largely from her oval face. Her skin was as white as the hottest star in their constellation called Salib, which Tsiera's people, the Ruhnits, called their eastern cross.

The Ruhnits had a special place in their hearts for their trinity of planets as it was foretold one would come that would serve the true path of justice. One would come that would serve the trinity of planets and the trinity of light. The Ruhnits had a prophet, Tsiera's father, whose dreams were as real as the arc Wahid walks by day. Unark the prophet, as the Ruhnits called him, foretold the day when the three suns of Al-Ruh, Wahid, the life giver, and Ithnaan and Thalaatha the twins would align, bringing Al-Wahid to save them from their dark deeds. Tsiera's *bug* glowed brightly now as she began her distance to the path before the sea. All around Tsiera, life glowed in response, and the path was bright for her to see.

Senate Office Building, Washington D.C.

Senator Buchanan from Kentucky, now the majority leader of the Republican controlled senate, read his private email. A hidden unhackable server had been installed in the secret compartment of his late 19th century oak desk. They spared no expense setting up his office when he won the election. The American Alliance never left one of their members without resources. Buchanan read the email with great interest and spoke out loud, "What are you up to, my dear Christian?"

"Sir?" spoke his rather young secretary from the outer office. Damn, thought the senator, I have to remember that new dictation microphone they added.

"Nothing Katrina, just thinking out loud," Kurt Buchanan had the device installed so Katrina could write his letters and give him the privacy needed to address the Alliance's business. What could the Pope possibly want with a star chart of Scorpius and the precise location of some star named Gleise? Oh well, the Church was always messing with the astronomers going back to Galileo. Odd thing though, the Church did not take away Galileo's instruments.

Now, this gold transaction on the valuable metals exchange bears closer scrutiny. This account number 6669996669992025 though missed by most computers snaking the data streams was not missed by the Alliance's Summit super computer using state of the art neural networks at its core. They had programmed it to look for anything remotely religious either Christian, Jewish, or Muslim in banking data streams. This Swiss account had grown from only a few million to 200 billion and growing exponentially overnight to over a trillion dollars back in 2011. I had better seek the truth of this, thought Kurt. Money in this quantity could be used to bring peace which is always bad for the economy. Thinking of the vast sum of money spent on the Summit computer, Kurt wondered why it had taken three years for this information to surface.

Peace would hamper the Alliance's plans to control the world until darkness could bring true justice. I will be rich beyond even the dreams of the Egyptians when darkness sweeps the land. Enough of caring for the poor and weak and downtrodden, enough of the free souls who sucked the life out of society, the truly free will wash the land with white supremacy. And maybe, just maybe, I can rape those Kentuckians of their last coal runs, and lick the thighs of their daughters after their men die of the black lung or succumb to other darker forces deep in the earth. The senator's mind wondered to the rather milky white thighs of his secretary whom he brought with him from Kentucky; not for her typing

abilities as they were subpar but for her ability to
distract those when needed with her physical attributes.

"Katrina love, take all my calls as I am headed out
for the evening. I have my AA meeting tonight." In
truth, AA was code for American Alliance and it was
nothing related to healing the souls of its members.

AA meeting, Washington, D.C.

"Our ranks are swelling with conservative Christians
who believe in our cause. Even more are waiting to
accept us as we pave the foundation of our conservative
dream. The layman's guard is forgotten as was foreseen
when the internet was expanded to include our
conservative call sites. We have thousands upon
thousands of middle class Americans believing that
fairness is only for them; only for those white men that
work hard for the American dream. The time has come

for us to put forth a new candidate that will bring true justice to our land and bring forth the darkness."

As Senator Buchanan spoke these words, the lights had dimmed noticeably and the shadows had grown across the room. In one corner, the shadows were particularly dark and one within moved and spread behind the senator. "We will convince these stupid Americans, blinding them with the chance to overturn Roe V. Wade bringing forth a savior that will pack the court with conservatory justices. All the while we will convince them it is ok to savor the taste of the flesh and degrade those that would seek to rule men. He will convince them to prey upon the weakness of those seeking a better life; those sniffling, lowly brown immigrants oozing up from the south, that still believe in all the commandments. He will embolden them to praise notes and cloth over their *righteous* God. He will support the eradication of one sin while he feeds their desires and have them embrace all the other sins impregnating their souls."

As the senator continued to speak with bile oozing from the corners of his mouth, the darkest shadow rose up and enveloped him absorbing into the very pores of his skin. "All the while praising the end of abortion, we will kill more souls across the land praising the hate of our neighbors, starving our children across the land, fondling and raping all the women to bear our offspring, putting our flag, our nation, above their God. I say, rise Patriots." As one, the white senators rose and began to sing, "*O say can you see, by the dawn's early light.*"

Chapter 3

In the year of our Lord 2014

The Vatican was in turmoil over the selection of Pope Vieira and the revolutionary visions he was beginning to put forth to the Church. Actually a very humble emissary from God put forth the very same visions as he walked the Earth some 2000 years earlier but that is a story for another time. Pope Vieira knew that his most revolutionary ideas would never see the light on Earth without ripping the Church into multiple factions. 2014 was a very different time with conservatives calling for support of the old ways but forgetting the very teachings of our Lord Jesus Christ. How quickly these conservatives read and then forgot His words, "Ye without sin, throw the first stone." Pope Vieira feared a holy war would begin anew. Unlike the war spawned by the words of Martin Luther, this war would forever destroy His true word. Pope Vieira had many allies but very few true friends, or so he thought, until he called a meeting in secret at the very tomb of Saint Peter.

"My friends, I have called you here today to hear the Word of God as spoken to me by the voice of an angel. He has allowed me to share this vision with you. To bless you to join His cause and to once again serve and follow in His footsteps, like our blessed Saint Peter did so many years ago," spoke Pope Vieira to the group of men and women gathered before him. "He has chosen me to begin this voyage of a new era, but once I place you on this path, I myself, must take a different path and continue His work here on the Earth."

Jake Young looked around at the group in this dimly lit chamber before the actual tomb of Saint Peter and almost laughed out loud at the melting pot of races gathered there. Within the chamber was a member of every race on Earth from every religion, and creed, and from every country in the world it would appear. He thought to himself, heck, I am one of the few white men here and probably one of the few Christians in the group.

"Doubt not that He speaks to you today," said Pope Vieira as Jake's thoughts were once again centered on his Holiness. Suddenly, every light in the room went out. At first, Jake thought the Vatican must be having a power outage, but then he could hear Mary Harrington, the English scientist speak out. "My flashlight also does not work," and then Abornazine Jones from the Native American tribe known as the Abenaki tribe, spoke, "No match will strike either." It was Hayat Muhammad who first noticed it. A faint glow began emanating from the tomb of Saint Peter. "Look," Hayat said as he pointed at the tomb. Suddenly, a brilliant light, unspeakably reverend, blazed from the tomb in the shape of a man.

The light rose as a person would rise from sleep and stood before them.

"My Lord, Jesus Christ, my friend, walked upon this Earth and gave me and my brothers the keys to heaven. What we blessed on this Earth will be blessed in Heaven, He said, and what we damned on Earth will remain damned for all eternity. His second coming is upon us, but my brothers and I have pleaded for one last chance for humanity. Before the wrath of God sweeps clean the land of my ancestors, you will have one last chance to follow the path of righteousness and truth. Your path does not lie before you here on Earth, however, but above you amongst the creation of Heaven. You will travel far and begin our flock anew. Your path will be fraught with danger, many will try to stop you, many will want to join you, but only the chosen may follow. Believe in His teachings, for they will not lead you astray. Drink from His cup as one."

The light slowly lowered back into the tomb and lay once again as if sleeping and slowly faded away.

Pope Vieira reached towards the tomb and pulled out of nothingness, His most Holy cup, the Grail of His last supper and said, *"This is the cup of my blood, the blood of the new and everlasting covenant. It will be shed for you and for all so that sins may be forgiven. Do this in memory of me."* Jake thought that many in the room would object, but at once all spoke "Amen" and received the blood of Christ and in doing so accepted the covenant which was laid before them. Pope Vieira spoke his final words to the group, "Upon accepting His covenant, you will return to your daily lives and speak of this no more until you are called. I have made ready the wealth of the entire Catholic world for your cause. The New Era, and our final trial, begins now. May God have mercy on our souls, if we should fail."

As the 100 souls left the tomb, members of the Militia Sancti Petri pulled aside a group of individuals

for a private meeting with his Holiness. Jake looked
around and thought he recognized a face but could not
place it. The man was lost in the group as they were
being hurried across the square. They were rushed into
Sala del Tronetto where the doors were locked behind
them as members of the Militia hurriedly seated the
group. As Jake scanned the room, he could see many of
the individuals he recognized from the tomb. One by
one they were all seated and Jake's eyes landed on the
individual directly across from him. Jake's adrenalin
began to rise as he recognized the man to be none other
than the Arab from the desert in Syria. Jake was still not
sure if this man was a friend or foe. Seated next to Jake
on his left was a british lady, Mary Harrington, from the
Vatican's observatory staff and on his right a native
American, Abornazine. Down towards the end of the
room not far from his Holiness, was a black priest who
looked familiar to Jake, though the beard was throwing
him off. Could that be Father Joe? Perhaps he was

mistaken as Father Joe from his old archdiocese back in Kentucky would have nothing to do with this gathering. Jake thought this was a rather odd mix of folks, but then this whole gathering was rather odd. His Holiness Pope Vieira entered the room. Jake was beginning to think he had made a mistake coming to this show and thought to leave. That option appeared to be lost as the Militia moved to lock and guard all the exits to the room. As his Holiness took the center high back chair at the end of the room, the room suddenly vibrated as a solid steel box lowered from the ceiling surrounding the seated individuals. Complete with lighting and a high tech audio video system, his Holiness began to speak.

"I must ask your forgiveness for all the security measures, and for the entire charade of gathering you here today. At this point, you must wonder if what you just witnessed was real or all some trick we play for tourists. I can assure you what we just experienced was very real. The question you should ask yourself is how does it fit your belief structure? And were you serious as you accepted the covenant or were you just playing along? As you may have gathered, not everyone in this room is of the same religion. So did those of you that are not Catholic just drink from the chalice for show?"

Members of the room begin to voice their objections at being called out on their lack of faith and many looked to leave though the box had no exits. His Holiness raised his hands and in his usual calming voice began to explain his vision. "My friends, my fellow believers, I will explain what we have all experienced and why you in particular have been called. Each of us has an undying faith in the creator but each of us has had many doubts since our birth about the written word. Abornazine, you call upon the Great Spirit. Mary, you call upon the spirit through your belief in Buddha. Hayat, you call upon Allah, and, Jake, you call upon our Catholic God. I am here today to tell you they are all one in the same. The spirit in the tomb just now was very real and is His essence here on Earth. What you do not realize but maybe have guessed at over the years is that the written word is very specific and tailored for Earth. Sadly, it has been twisted and used to fit our needs and to justify our actions however reprehensible. I will tell you now; I am His true emissary here on Earth. Past popes have simply been figureheads appointed by men of the Catholic Church. As his emissary here on earth, God has spoken to me. It is time to spread the word beyond the Earth. As the shadows have continued to spread throughout the land turning us against one another, God has decided to let this experiment on Earth play out but begin again out there amongst the stars."

As his Holiness spoke, the walls of the steel box began to display stars very familiar to many in the room. "We have all questioned our existence in the universe and tried to reconcile the written word with what our very eyes see above us every clear night. It is not against His word to believe there is more beyond

our planet. It is not blasphemy to believe God is more

than what civilizations have written down on papyrus

for eons. I am here to tell you now that we are not alone

in the universe. It is time to spread His word yet again

as it has been done for millennia."

"You have all been called here to take yet again, a

leap of faith, and build something that will take us

beyond our world to a world located here." The display

began to zoom from the Scorpius constellation down to

a very red star.

Mary Harrington gasped out loud and began to

speak. "Forgive me, your Holiness. Even if I can come

to terms with what you are asking us to believe, I must

speak out. That planetary system does not exist. What

we thought I had proven had planets around it was

determined to be noise in our readings. The light

fluctuations from the other stars in the system fooled us,

fooled me, into believing we were seeing transits. I lost

my grant over that system and was ridiculed for even publishing my results. How can you..."

Pope Vieira rose from his chair and walked over to Mary to place his hands on her shoulders. "Mary, I must beg your forgiveness. We, the Church, owned your research grant. As you took those detailed measurements, we were recording them here. We added the noise using the Cross, our supercomputer, humming even now beneath this very building. Your research, your work, we covered up." Pope Vieira kneeled at her feet and spoke, "Mary, forgive me. The planets are there, right where you said they would be. It was necessary to guard this system from others and from the shadows for as long as possible, so we could spread His Word again beyond our world. So we would have a system for the journey I have called, He has called, you here for today."

Tears began to crawl down Mary's cheeks reddened by her embarrassment of speaking out. In her eyes, though, could be seen a twinkle of hope, and the beginnings of forgiveness. Mary reached out to touch the cheek of his Holiness and spoke ever so quietly, "Kyrie eleison, is this possible?"

"Mary, Jake, Abor, Joe, Hayat," His Holiness began to speak the names of every individual in the room addressing them directly. "I can assure you this is very real, and He will have mercy on us as Ms. Mary has so eloquently spoken. Faith has been over relied upon for thousands of years on our planet. As we travel this road together, I will begin to give you a bit more than just faith as I provide some evidence for His plan. For today however, we have much work to begin. I am afraid I must ask you to rely on your faith in His Spirit to get us started."

Chapter 4

22 light-years away on Al-Ruh as Wahid begins to give way to the night

Unark began his Khutba, his sermon, at the end of Wahid's walk of arc this day as he had done for hundreds of Al-Ruh's paths. He called upon the great Al-Wahid to bless the life of Al-Ruh and all Ruhnits. As he continued, he could see his daughter, Tsiera, descending from the path as Wahid left its last rays upon her feet and Al-Ruh pitched into total darkness.

"This passing of Wahid, all Ruhnits have suffered the depths of darkness once again. We have seen khitayana spread and open the wells of Al-Wahid to rain upon us. Damu has been spilled amongst us and the dhilal are spreading to darken our hearts. Blood and shadows will forever darken our hearts until he, Al-Wahid, visits upon us and forgives khitayana. Al-Wahid has spoken to me that he will come within fifty cycles of the dance of the twins, Ithnaan and Thalaatha. We must prepare the passage and assign one amongst us to take my place to continue the way of the truth and the light."

As Tsiera joined the group, and took her place next to her father, all Ruhnits rose as one calling her name, "Tsiera! Tsiera! Tsiera!" Tsiera had been born with an unsual gift on Al-Ruh. Hayita Tsiera Bakineret was born with no shadow and could bring to life all fluorescents on Al-Ruh. Tsiera looked upon her father as her eyes traced the lines of Wahid's passage upon the face of her father. Tears filled his large oval eyes as they beamed with pride for his daughter. She thought, though, she could see something of sadness in those loving eyes....or was it fear. She wondered what else Unark had kept from her and the rest of the Ruhnits of his dreams for the future. No matter now as she was committed to serve.

Tsiera took her place at the stone next to her father and began to glow. The florescence she could command began to emanate from her body as instantly she became a blazing blue orb. "Fellow Ruhnits, prepare and mark well your khitayana. As my father has seen, I too have seen His face. We must mark the dance of Ithnaan and Thalaatha and begin the cleansing of dhilal from our lands.".

Pandere Aerospace Headquarters

"Your Holiness, it will be done as you have requested. All modules are in preparation now at our private facility." Mr. Pandere was preparing to be a very rich, if mostly forgotten man, who at one point had great dreams. A smile spread across his face as he began to realize that not all dreams were meant to be flaunted. His pride had almost destroyed him until his

Holiness Pope Vieira had sent his emissary, Monsignor Mike, to open his eyes to the light.

"Bill!" his Holiness spoke to demand his attention once more. "My forgiveness, your Holiness, I've had wondering thoughts these last few months with a lack of sleep from the preparations. As you have requested, our stocks have been slowly losing value and we are preparing to file for bankruptcy to cover the activities. To the outside world, it will appear that the expandable spacecraft was just another failed venture. We are still waiting for the key life environment mechanics and navigations, as well as this propulsion drive you have mentioned. I trust you still have faith it will work?"

"Bill, you still do not have the faith of your childhood I can see. Ours is a lonely path but as He has spoken to me, Abor's drive will work. The idea was buried so the shadows could spread destruction and fuel the end. It will work! Even now the unit is being prepared to ship to your facility for assembly."

Bill's mind began to wander again as he remembered when Monsignor Mike had first approached him with this crazy idea. But, he had the money to pay for the entire fiasco and Bill's company was not at a point where he could turn down such a proposal. Pandere was at a sink or swim moment and he was not one to drown if he could help it.

"Bill Pandere are you listening to me?" his Holiness spoke loudly to snap Bill out of his lost thoughts.

"Yes, your Holiness, I'm here."

"Bill, the team will be arriving at the end of this week to finalize the criticals of the mission. We must meet the launch window for assembly, as we need to cover the activity with NASA's gateway construction. I trust the Militia Sancti Petri have already secured the facility?"

"Yes, they have been here for some time now. Not even Satan himself could get past their screening and the lockdown of our private facility."

His Holiness paused and thought that perhaps just this once he could hope Bill was correct. "Bill, my trusted friend, may He bless you with eternal happiness for your work and may He bless us with a safe period to continue our operations into the heavens."

One week later
Pandere Aerospace private facility

Buried deep beneath the sands of Las Vegas, the Pope's chosen few had convened for a final design review of what would be the construction of the largest spaceship known to humankind, the NUERA1. The first spacecraft designed for interstellar travel and fully funded by a religious organization, none other than the Catholic Church. Pope Vieira taking advantage of a visit to Las Vegas to chastise the establishments for their procreation of sins of the flesh had set aside time to meet with the group before component launch.

"Many of you have met only in passing and with some of you not necessarily on the best of terms," as his Holiness glanced towards Jake Young and Hayat Muhammad. "I can assure you we are all friends here and doing His work. I must explain to you now the talents of each gathered here today. As you know, we are leaving Earth, well; at least a chosen few of you are leaving. Some of the best minds working on great ideas long forgotten were plucked from their deteriorating lives to bring forth these ideas to fruition once more. You see, nothing He commands has ever been wasted. You may wonder about the importance of those in this room. I can assure you they are all needed. The final modules of NUERA1 are here before us thanks in sum to the talents of each of you. Bill, can you take over and cover the details briefly?"

Bill Pandere took center stage, well, center of the concrete floor anyway, to begin in detail as a screen dropped from the steel trusses across the ceiling of the vast building. "I will try not to bore you with the minutia but limit my discussion to the broader topics important to the final testing of the last modules and, of course, what you need to know to take this monumental leap into the stars. Be assured that your safety and the safety of all 100 initial crew and compliment of NUERA1 have been taken into consideration. The very idea, the very basic concept of the craft you will travel in, live in, began back in the early 60's with the launch of Echo 2. An expandable craft capable of housing a few instruments has now become a carefully crafted module utilizing the benefits of Kevlar. As you can see from the display, a multi-layer inflatable shell LAY-UP will become...."

As Mr. Pandere's voice trailed off in Jake's mind, he wondered exactly how an engineer defined minutia.

Jake had wondered up to this point why they needed a

fighter pilot for this mission of his Holiness, as the

Vatican did not have fighter aircraft. It was not until a

few weeks back had he been given the full title of his

new position in this motley group, "Jake Young, you

will be Commander Young and pilot of NUERA1," his

Holiness spoke during their last secret meeting at the

Vatican. Jake had been having serious misgivings about

his whole involvement in this charade of the Pope's.

Somehow the Pope had arranged for him to be released

several months early from his commitment with the Air

Force. Jake's Catholic faith had sorely suffered since he

left that the little country church in Kentucky. He

always had a great commitment to doing the right thing

but something, some memory, had always darkened his

thoughts when it came to the Church. His attendance at

the gathering at the tomb of Saint Peter was more of a

way to get some free travel time than any real solid

belief in Catholicism, yet something deep within Jake's

soul moved him as well. Being pulled from the Air Force had also had the misfortune of ending his retirement pension early and now Jake again wondered why the Church was meddling in his affairs.

That night in his apartment a few weeks prior, Jake tried to settle in for a night of restless sleep; a side effect of his long missions on oxygen the Air Force doc always told him. Jake had made up his mind to tell the Pope he was through with this game. Jake tossed and turned until finally fitfully dropping into a bombing run on some unnamed village. His dream began to change. Jake found himself back in 5th grade at his old church's backstage. A game, Jake thought at first, as the Catholic fat man had told them it would be fun. The fat man began to roll across Jake and he felt smothered lying on the stage floor. He could not breath, could not catch his breath from the weight of the 400 lb man as he rolled across Jake shaking up and down. Jake tried to yell stop, tried to say "I cannot breath" as panic began to set in. He felt himself losing consciousness and wet himself as he mouthed the word "Stopppppp!!!!".

Jake awoke with a start, soaked through with sweat, frozen still from the nightmare, afraid to move. Across the room, there he was, the angel from the desert of Syria, Archangel Michael, with his sword pulled and blazing beside him. Jake slowly sat up beginning to regain some movement from the paralysis of his nightmare. "Do not get up on my behalf, young Jake, as His dreams can take one some time to fully recover from," as the Archangel Michael moved to place his sword on Jake's shoulder.

"You mean He purposely caused me to remember that! I've gone for 20 years burying that deep away to never remember it. Why? Why would He bring forth that agony? It is not enough I lost my faith, I lost my wife and child to those nightmares. I had just begun to think recovery, redemption, forgiveness....was possible."

"Jake what He did, what He did through me, was necessary. You were beginning to have doubts in his Holiness' cause. We need you, Jake; He needs you, to fight the darkness as the shadows even now are threatening to destroy your kind. He has great plans for you, Jake. You must understand even darkness can bring light. Past popes and many in the Church have been guilty of great evil, great darkness, to many young souls. They will receive His judgment in good time. First, He will use their darkness, their despicable greed, their unholy piousness to achieve His ends upon this world. I am here to give you a glimpse of the next world where He will spread the light."

Jake could not remember many of the scenes presented to his mind that night, but the image of the alien girl glowing subtly in blue stuck with him. It was as if all darkness had been abolished and he was looking at the true light of God. She smiled at him and spoke, "Mudamir Alshari-Destroyer of evil."

"Each of the modules of NUERA1 will be protected with the outer skin based upon the Multi-Layer Inflatable shell LAY-UP providing you the latest protection against micrometeorite impacts, from the vacuum of space, fire, and internal protection from within the unit." Mr. Pandere continued with his detailed explanation of all the modules and their functions. "The space station will be divided into three main sections or wings, the tourist wing, the science wing, and Command, Control, and Communications (CCC). There will also be a super sized module similar in size to Pandere's Olympus module with a volume of 2100 cubic meters. The *tourist wing* will consist of two main inflatable modules, one for living quarters and one for the microgravity fun zone. The science wing will also consist of two main inflatable modules, one for living quarters and one for the microgravity research lab. Both the microgravity fun zone and the research lab will consist of 581 cubic meters. In all, the station layout will consist of seven inflatable modules (4 standard units x 330 cubic meters, 2 extended units x 581 cubic meters, and one Olympus style unit at 2100 cubic meters), eight nodes x 78 cubic meters, and ten cupolas x 6 cubic meters, a propulsion module, and fourteen permanent crew transportation vehicles (CTVs) for a total of 5266 cubic meters of usable volume. NUERA1 will have well over 5 times the pressurized volume of the International Space Station."

Dr. Mary Harrington, who until this point had remained very quite, spoke up, "Ah, Mr. Pandere, we are talking about sending at least 100 individuals on this voyage, I do not see how we can possibly have enough volume. And did you say a tourist wing? Is this an escape vehicle or a tourist attraction?"

"Well as you can see, Dr. Harrington, we have to lead with the subterfuge that this is a low Earth orbit vessel designed for just that, tourists, and some low level research. This is necessary in case these plans were to fall into the wrong hands. I will only mention here verbally that when your voyage is ready to leave the Earth system, two Nautilus style gravity modules will have been attached expanding your capacity. Thanks to my colleagues, Mark Holderman and Edward Henderson, an old design will finally see the light of day."

"Dr. Harrington, may I call you Mary?" Bill began to drop the more serious engineering tone of his talk to speak on a more personal level.

Mary spoke up, "Yes, please by all means. After all, it is your company's designs we are relying upon for our very survival."

"Yes Mary, as well as some key contributions from members of your group not yet explained in detail to you. Dr. Abor Jones please stand. Dr. Abornazine Jones's thorium reactor and drive will provide the propulsion as well as the power for your vessel. Abor's full name means keeper of the flame and I can assure you as your resident nuclear engineer on board, he

intends to do just that. And let's see, oh yes, in the back,

Dr. Hayat Muhammad, please stand. Dr. Muhammad's

ECLSS, your environmental control and life support

system with a few tweaks, will keep you all alive and

well fed for the journey. Dr. Harrington, Mary, as you

know is our astrophysicist, and navigator for this

journey. Over here to my left is Jake Young,

Commander Jake Young, your captain and pilot. And

here to my right, is Father Joseph Washington or some

may refer to him as Dr. Joseph Washington, your

resident therapist, psychiatrist, and all around keeper of

your souls. Joe will be responsible for many things, but

you can also refer to him as your morale officer. Abor, I

believe you know Father Joe from your parish?" Abor

looked over to see the grey bearded man with sudden

recognition on his face. Father Joe had aged far beyond

his years. Ah, but perhaps the beard added to the affect.

Strange he had not noticed during their last meeting

with the Pope. Bill spoke again, "Welcome all, as this is your first full personal introduction and technical gathering of the crew of NUERA1. You will all need to depend on the skills of everyone in this room for NUERA1 to survive the journey to Gliese."

Chapter 5

In the year of our Lord 2018

Senator Kurt Buchanan rose to the podium with longer lines on his face and a noticeable paunch protruding from his belt. Those present could no longer see, but his skin was grey as the darkness spread within. "My friends and fellow Patriots, it is with great honor that we celebrate Grave West's acceptance as leader of the National Rifle Association. Even now, our ranks are boiling over in all areas of our great democracy. Grave has sealed the deal as we continue to infiltrate all areas of society with the weapons needed to take back what is the God given right of the white man. This great land was ours for the taking. God gave us the Negro to use and the slant eyed Asians to build our great empire upon their worthless backs. We wiped the disease from this great land. The heathen indians are now regulated to the bowels of the worthless areas of our nation. Oh yes, the darkies tried to rise up, but our friend Grave helped us beat them back down with their own addictions."

Kurt's thoughts trailed to his meeting last night with his secretary, Katrina. He had used the same addiction to force her to satisfy his hunger time and time again in their hotel room. Spreading the white powder all over his body she licked and sucked and snorted until eventually succumbing to the powers of the white god. It would not be long before her time was finished and he would need to pull another coal miner's daughter up from Kentucky. As yellow grey slime oozed from the corners of Senator Kurt's mouth, he shook himself back to the moment at hand. "It is with great honor and humility, that I announce to you my fellow Patriots, you blessed members of our American Alliance, that I will be publicly announcing my candidacy for President of these United States for the next term." As one, the members rose, wild eyed with darkness in their eyes, yelling as one, "Buchanan for President!" as Senator Kurt Buchanan left the podium.

Walking back to his hotel room, his phone rings, surprising Kurt from his dark thoughts of ruling the world. "Sir, we received the information that you have requested concerning the activities of the Vatican and his Holi... I mean Antonio's activities." Katrina spoke cautiously as she realized she slipped when using the name of honor given to the Pope as that could rile the senator.

"Go on girl, spit it out!" Kurt spoke bluntly.

"Sir, the individuals that have been meeting seem to be working on some things to improve the environment. That Hayat Muhammad is working with human feces to create a fertilizer and Abor Jones is still playing around with his thorium drive with no great success. As you predicted, nobody will want to support nuclear power that cannot be weaponized. The rest of the group are has-beens from various walks of life, an aging priest, a pilot that quit the Air Force, and some lady that worked at the Vatican's observatory in Arizona. They could see nothing consequential for your plans. It appears the space was rented in the old factory of Pandere for their meeting."

"Ok, love, tell them to continue to monitor Antonio but spend limited resources as I have great plans for my upcoming election," spoke the Senator as he considered his next steps to ruling the masses. Though, something nagged him deep in the back of his mind about the priest. What was it about Father Joe? It was quickly forgotten as the Senator looked forward to his evening activities with Katrina.

A small town in Kentucky

It was a late winter day in Kentucky where the temperatures teased of spring. Though the sun had risen over an hour ago, the sheets of rain pouring down and the dark clouds covered this fact. The congregation sat down as they prepared to hear the last words of Father Joseph Washington. Word had spread fast as it does in small towns even before Father Joe could officially announce it. He was leaving their small parish to continue the work of their Pope elsewhere. Father Joe, signed the cross, and rose to the podium. The parishioners had not noticed that some of their flock were already missing these past few months. Abor Jones and his family had not been to Sunday mass in some time. Father Joe's beard had turned solid white in stark contrast to his dark features. He looked older than his years, but the fire was still in his eyes. Some even noticed that there was something else there this morning. Perhaps there was a sparkle of hope?

"My friends, as some of you probably know, the Archdiocese has decided to send me elsewhere to serve his Holiness. I will leave within the month to serve on a committee to address the stark divides that have crept through the world dividing even Christians from His good work. Today we will address some of these divides with the hope that perhaps a few will listen."

"My brothers and sisters of all faiths, we are falling. Satin is laughing; we have fallen so far. Not just a little snicker mind you, but a real rolling belly laugh from the bowels of hell. He is laughing so hard, you can feel the vibrations across the world. We have forgotten our roots, buried them deep beyond understanding. The greatest nation under God; we have become the greatest nation of hypocrites."

"Matthew 23, *Then Jesus said to the crowds and to his disciples: 'The teachers of the law and the Pharisees sit in Moses' seat. So you must be careful to do everything they tell you. But do not do what they do, for they do not practice what they preach. They tie up heavy, cumbersome loads and put them on other people's shoulders, but they themselves are not willing to lift a finger to move them. Everything they do is done for people to see...Woe to you, teachers of the law and Pharisees, you hypocrites! You clean the outside of the cup and dish, but inside they are full of greed and self-indulgence. Woe to you, teachers of the law and Pharisees, you hypocrites! You are like whitewashed tombs, which look beautiful on the outside but on the inside are full of the bones of the dead and everything unclean. In the same way, on the outside you appear to people as righteous but on the inside you are full of hypocrisy and wickedness."'*

Father Joe continued with conviction, "Oh yes, we established this great country with noble words. Perhaps you are familiar with the Constitution of the United States Preamble. *We the People of the United States, in Order to form a more perfect Union, establish*

Justice, insure domestic Tranquility, provide for the common defence, promote the general Welfare, and secure the Blessings of Liberty to ourselves and our Posterity, do ordain and establish this Constitution for the United States of America."

The congregation, used to Father Joe's history lessons, was a little taken back by his sermon this morning. "We even established a great Bill of Rights. I will only highlight two here to make my point. The first amendment says: *Congress shall make no law respecting an establishment of religion, or prohibiting the free exercise thereof; or abridging the freedom of speech, or of the press; or the right of the people peaceably to assemble, and to petition the government for a redress of grievances.* Our second amendment says, *A well regulated militia, being necessary to the security of a free state, the right of the people to keep and bear arms, shall not be infringed.* Oh my friends and followers of Christ, we started off on the right foot but with total disregard for the teachings of our Lord and Savior Jesus Christ. He warned us then of our failings; foreshadowed our weaknesses, yet we failed to listen, to heed the words. Now we want to display a puppet of the government, this Grave West, as our spokesperson for supporting the 2nd amendment, hypocrites we are all."

"This morning I have brought a guest to help me with the homily. Some of you may even recognize this man as he was a past parishioner here. Jake Young will be serving with me and others for his Holiness in the upcoming months and years. Please give him your undivided attention and respect as you would me."

"Good Morning folks, though most of you I do not recognize, I do remember the family names. Know that I speak with respect for our Lord and Savior. Though I serve in another capacity now, there was a time I considered the cloth. Father Joe asked me to speak to the canyons of divisions that have separated us recently, but these have been here for centuries. The darkness has blinded us to His teachings. We judge when we should not and this has become even more evident in recent days with one man praying on bended knee. How easy it is for us to go watch a few movies or read a few books and shed a tear for the black man or woman and feel like we understand. We grew up with black friends or at least we called them friends, but did we understand how they felt? Did we understand what they felt? Some of us worked alongside them in the hay fields, but did we know what it meant to be black? We went to school with them and played with them at recess, but did we really know them? Did I know their pain, their suffering, and their hearts? How could we? We were white. How could I? I am white. This country supported their enslavement. Our ancestors killed one another during the Civil War to free them but only in words. Our ancestors claimed to be followers of Christ on Sunday but still enslaved them again behind closed doors in secret. We had a cure for Syphilis but withheld it for forty years adding another forty years of enslavement. The biggest irony of all is the very president that apologized for their treatment helped to distract our attention and the media's attention from another travesty. While he played around with cigars in the White House, another scandal was trying to come out. Sadly, America cared all too much about cigars at the time. Yes, there is plenty of evidence out there now to support this claim. We knew where the money was coming from to pay for the Contras; we just did not care. I mean after all, we were only enslaving black people to a drug our own government helped to refine. And we think Grave West knew nothing of where the money was coming from to support this illegal war. Strange how we ignore what we do not want to know."

"I remember a time when I practiced swearing an oath studying and working to become an officer in the Air Force as a member of Detachment 220, the Air

Force Reserve Officers training core at Purdue University. *I, Jake Young, having been appointed a 1st lieutenant in the United States Air Force, do solemnly swear that I will support and defend the Constitution of the United States against all enemies, foreign and domestic; that I will bear true faith and allegiance to the same; that I take this obligation freely, without any mental reservation or purpose of evasion; and that I will well and faithfully discharge the office upon which I am about to enter. So help me God."*

"I took all of this very seriously and even went as far as pledging and becoming a member of the Arnold Air Society. My fellow cadets were all very serious and willing to die for a cause. There were Blacks, Whites, and Asians in my cadet class; every single one my brother and sister. We believed we were going to take the real oath one day as officers in the Air Force; the oath to defend the Constitution of the United States. My fellow cadets, some still serving in the Air Force today, took the oath and what it meant to heart. We talked about this, defending the Constitution of the United States, and what the Constitution stood for. We fully understood we would be defending freedom. Not just the freedom we liked, but most importantly the freedom we did not. It has been said many times and many ways that it only takes one good man to look the other way for evil to grab a foothold. I cannot in good faith to my Lord stay silent. I thank God and Father Joe for giving me a chance to speak out today. Many of us post in social media about wanting to keep our second amendment; forgetting the amendment that came first. We forget why a second amendment was seen as paramount to protecting the first. I will repeat the 1st amendment again for those of us who have forgotten."

"The first amendment states *Congress shall make no law respecting an establishment of religion, or prohibiting the free exercise thereof; or abridging the freedom of speech, or of the press; or the right of the people peaceably to assemble, and to petition the government for a redress of grievances*. Need I translate this for those of us that have forgotten? It basically states Congress cannot create a law supporting any religion over another. Congress cannot create a law prohibiting any religion. Congress cannot create a law that would take away our right of free speech or the right of free press. Congress cannot create a law that prohibits peaceful assembly, nor can they create a law that would prevent us from petitioning the government."

"You know I remember my oath well. So help me God. Above all, I took the oath to God to defend those that cannot defend themselves. If a man or a woman wants to kneel during the national anthem to protest the treatment of his or her brothers and sisters, I support them. I have taken an oath. If he or she wants to spit, stomp, defecate, etc. on the very flag of his or her, my country, out of protest, I support them, though it may pain me to watch. It may anger me near to the breaking point. It is just a song; it is just a flag. They are absolutely worthless artifacts of nationalism if the words they represent mean nothing. We break the very commandment we have made with God putting a few notes and a piece of cloth before Him. Folks, I am but a child of God. I was not raised to be a racist. These were my friends. These are my friends; Liz, Bridget, Lamont, Stephen, Rod, Victor, Lillian, Denise, Craig, Father Joe and so many more. I never once asked or even considered what it was like to be black. I can no longer stand by and stand silent as darkness continues to sweep our country and our world."

"I have killed many innocents from the cockpit all for a few notes and bit of cloth. For that, He will judge me, but I will work the last of my days to earn His forgiveness. It is not just the blacks that those white Patriots have forsaken for their worship of a false god. They have tried and all but succeeded in wiping the

Native Americans from the face of our country. They have convinced many of you that if you are a Muslim, Jew, Hindu, Buddhist, or anything but a white Christian, you cannot seek the path of righteousness. If your skin is not white, you are lesser of a human. We have looked the other way. We have turned our eyes from God and mark my words, the evil darkness, has gained a foothold in these states of America. On the very flag we raised for our state of Kentucky, we marked the words *United We Stand, Divided We Fall*. These states are united no more and we are falling. My friends, my old neighbors, when we tell another person when they can and cannot pray to God, we have crossed the line. We have placed ourselves and a few notes and a bit of cloth between that person and God. As Father Joe spoke the words of His Son Jesus, we are hypocrites. There is a chance for some of us and in God, there is always hope. I am honored to work with Father Joe and others to see an end to the darkness that is dividing what was once a great country and the rest of the world."

Jake realized as he spoke that more than a few in the congregation had stepped out the back door, skipping even their Holy Communion to avoid hearing his words. He knew from what his Holiness Pope Vieira had said that for many it was too late. The darkness had consumed them to the point of no return. It was this way all over the Earth, congregation after congregation was succumbing to the ways of the dark path. The time was upon us for a battle not seen upon the Earth since the giants roamed. Jake's new role as captain and commander of NUERA1 had taken on new importance and he prayed to God that day to give him and the rest of the crew the strength to carry forward.

Chapter 6

Al-Ruh in the time of Zalazil

Abu, Ibn, and Al-Ruh danced around Wahid an average of every 33 days, Al-Ruh completing the circuit every 21 days, Ibn, 30 days, and Abu almost 39 days. Tsiera knew, as most Ruhnits, that when the twins ruled the darkness and glowed upon the land that the zalazil would return and continue giving them life upon the land. Though the little ones of Al-Ruh had not learned this yet, their eyes glowed with excitement as preparations were made for the grand celebration of alhaya, life, on Al-Ruh. This passing, Unark, with assistance from Tsiera, would tell the story again as they had for so many passings. All the little ones twitched and bounced up front of the outdoor meeting area barely waiting in anticipation of Tsiera's grand entrance. For on this night, Tsiera would represent Wahid in all its glory.

Unark took his place upon the stone and began the story of what sustained alhaya on Al-Ruh. "Wise Ruhnits from many passings ago studied the dance of our trinity around Wahid. With their knowledge, we now understand why life is possible around our entire world of Al-Ruh. Within a few arcs of Wahid, we will experience the zalazil, the quakes, that sustain our world and keep it temperate for our survival. Without zalazil, our elders learned the trinity would be doomed to always face Wahid causing an unbalance in life upon these worlds."

As Unark continued, the little ones' already enlarged eyes grew perceptibly larger as their mouths gapped open to behold the site blazing forth from outside their seating area. Tsiera entered the gathering blazing her light forward as the twin sisters of Ruhnit glowed behind her using *bugs* from the land to simulate their

stars. Three brothers from their tribe danced around
Tsiera to simulate the passing of the trinity planets in
their system. They danced and fell to the ground to roll
and then would bounce up again to dance some more.
Slowly from the distance drums could be heard
rumbling forth. The sisters pulled out more glowing
orbs to bring forth the full magnitude of the twin stars
to light as they ruled the night. The brother's dance
became even more flamboyant as they now would jump
up onto some empty stones, fall to the ground, and
dance some more grasping hands and spinning rapidly
around Tsiera as her light blazed even brighter. The
drums could now not only be heard but also felt as they
began to pulse together. The little ones looked a bit
panicked as the very stones they sat upon began to
vibrate to the pulse of the drums. As the drums would
beat together, BOOM, the brothers would flip head over
heels, and spin again around Tsiera. The drums would
beat together again, BOOM, and the stones upon which

the little ones sat even bounced a bit off the ground. Of course, unbeknownst to the little ones, Unark's friends had installed a bit of theatrics to help the stones along. One tiny little one had enough and ran to her giver of life with some tears in her eyes. Unark frowned at her mother as there was an age limit for this celebration. Not to be subdued by the tears, Unark's voice began to join the drums beating as one, "Zalazil, Zalazil, Zalazil!" All the little ones at this point could no longer stay seated upon their stones and were rolling themselves on the ground. Suddenly at once, Unark and the drums stopped and Unark strode forth with Tsiera, the twin sisters, and the brothers to the front of the gathering.

Unark began his speech of preparation, "As we have done for so many zalazils, we must prepare our humble abodes. Tie down your wall coverings, pack and store your fragilities, and bring forth your contributions to the celebration to take place in three days. Remember during zalazil all will live outdoors and gather and sleep in the open meadows. As you may remember, a few young Ruhnits last zalazil thought they could ride out the quakes." Unark gently rapped the three brothers on their heads scolding them for their foolishness. "It took many passings of the arc of Wahid to heal their wounds and I suspect many more to heal their pride. Remember their foolishness and guard your minds to such thoughts as it is very dangerous not to heed my words." Unark good-naturedly rubbed the fuz on the brothers' heads, what little hair cover Ruhnits actually had, and thanked them for their participation in the zalazil preparation play.

In the year of our Lord 2024
Safford, Arizona

Dr. Mary Harrington was wrapping up her work at the Vatican Advanced Technology Telescope near Safford, AZ. The data she had access to now from the Cross was teasing out a few details hidden from the rest of the world. Tonight she brought along the rest of the crew of NUERA1 to explain what she had resolved to understand could be the only explanation for the data she was reviewing. The Cross had been tasked with running simulations using the data recently gathered by a radio telescope just now coming to life on the far side of the moon. The soon to be commissioned, Saptarshi Bandyopadhyay Radio Telescope, had been testing old theories from data gathered from the LOFAR radio telescope in the Netherlands. Pope Vieira was leaving no stone unturned and had given Mary access to all instruments available to confirm their destination was a valid survivable planet. Scientists had long been concerned that if a planet orbiting close to a red dwarf did not have a sufficient magnetic field, it could not block the intense radiation from the interaction of the planet with the red dwarf star. The solar winds from the red giant would fry the planet with radiation making it uninhabitable.

As Mary began to speak, she rubbed the belly of the Buddha neckless that never left her neck. Some who might notice would think it was a good luck charm, but it was Mary's way of reminding herself of her past efforts at Samadhi, concentration and meditation. It calmed her spirit as she was always nervous at talking in front of crowds and even small groups such as this.

"I have gone over the simulations with the Cross one hundred times and the result is always the same. The third planet in the system does indeed have a strong magnetic field. So strong in fact we will need to make some modifications to the onboard radiation shielding of NUERA1 to protect the ship as we enter the system. However, the very essence of this field is necessary to protect life on the planet from the intense radiation of

Gliese 667C. I have given the necessary data to Mr. Pandere and the onboard field is being modified now to protect us and our passengers for entry into the system. We also have some exciting news out of Chile. I do not even begin to understand his Holiness' sway with the scientific community especially the astronomical community. Perhaps with Chile having a population of over 50% Catholic, he has some pull. No matter, but we should be thankful to God as we now have confirmation our destination also has liquid water - oceans of liquid water. The Extremely Large Telescope (ELT) in the Atacama Desert has had it's first light a bit early. Though not scheduled to come online for another year, his Holiness was able to convince them to image our new home. I will not bore you with the details, but an old collegue of mine, Jacob Lustig-Yaeger, and others have been able to see the glint of light off the oceans of Gliese 667C (c)."

A collective sigh of relief was heard across the group and a glint of hope could easily be seen in all the eyes of the group. Though the crew of NUERA1 had faith and it had been tested already several times, it never hurts to have cold hard facts to boost morale. Mary continued, "I am sure you also realize that measuring a periodic glint also proves the planet is not tidally locked. As we theorized, the location of the trinity of planets and their respective gravitational pulls on one another would prevent this from happening. We do know that this also means our new world will be a bit shaky at times."

Abor looked up at Mary from his deep thoughts on optimizing his thorium drive with a puzzled look, "What do you mean by shaky?"

Jake elbowed Abor and said, "You are not afraid of a few quakes are you, Abor?"

The group over the last few years had come together with a strong sense of camaraderie. Jake's military background had served him well in his role as captain and commander. With Father Joe and Jake working together they had devised a way to unite this group of odd ball scientists, a priest, and two military officers into a unit working as one for the goal of God. Perhaps not the God they were raised to believe in from their individual religions but the God that in reality did exist. With some old fashion sweat and a bit of blood, they whipped the group together in better physical shape than they ever would have believed. They were not a fighting military unit as Jake would continually remind himself, but they needed to work together as if their lives depended on one another and in space this would be tested time and time again. Jake and Hayat were not yet friends, but they were *friendly* and dedicated to the cause. Either one would defend the other to the death in support of their mission. Abor, who was becoming a strong member of the team, seemed a bit dark and troubled at times. Jake could not put a finger on it, but thought perhaps it was commonplace for engineers and scientists to get moody, especially when their theories were being put to the test. Jake looked over at Abor and thought today perhaps was one of those days.

Abor looked darker and gloomier than usual as he worked his figures only half listening to Mary's announcements. It was his turn next to give his report on propulsion and power. Abor rose as he continued to work equations on his clipboard but finally placed it back on his seat. He knew the answer for many months and supposed Pope Vieira and perhaps others knew this as well. "Ok, I have put together my report for today but," Abor paused as he heard the door to the conference room open, and his Holiness entered surrounded by security from the Militia Sancti Petri. All but Jake looked surprised as Pope Vieira entered and went to stand beside Abor. Antonio, as he had asked them to address him, placed his hand on Abor's shoulder and simply spoke, "Let me, my son." Abor sat back down with some relief easily showing on his tan red face. Antonio could not hide his years as he stooped over with a crook in his back. He knew that he would be the last pope in a long line to serve the Catholic Church. His last service to God would be this mission. He spoke with sadness but also with confidence in the dedication of his followers.

"It is good to see you all gathered here today. I see you all look very fit and if I might add even a bit younger if that is possible. I should not delay further what I think some of you have possibly guessed at and poor Abor here has sullied over for many months. Even God has limits in what can be divulged to us and I am afraid faster than light speed of course is not one of those items we shall know. Of course you knew that, but I'm not sure you realized that even with Abor's thorium drive, speeds over half a light year will also not be possible. We are limited once again my friends to the trinity of three. At most you will achieve one third the speed of light. Even at that speed it will take 63 years to get to your destination. However, you also have to be able to slow down to capture yourself into orbit around the planet. Abor's drive will speed you up and then you will rotate the ship and use it to slow you down, but we estimate it will take approximately 126 years to reach your new home. Yes, NUERA1 is a generation ship."

Chapter 7

In the year of our lord 2024

Campaign headquarters for President-Elect

Buchanan

The hour was way past midnight as the election results for most states had already been decided. President-Elect Buchanan sat on the sofa inebriated from the Kentucky whiskey he had passed out for celebration. Katrina was slumbering next to him a bit high with the extra special something Kurt had added to her drink. She long ago had stopped trying to keep her breasts from spilling out of her blouse. Kurt eyed them now as he could easily see all the bounties he had been given on this day. Tonight he brought out something different as he pulled the syringe. He would have his way with Katrina one last time as her usefulness had come to an end. As he reached down to grab her wrist, Katrina mumbled "No, Kurt, I mean President-Elect...," but then nodded off to lose consciousness. Kurt opened the security app on his phone and checked all the cameras one more time to ensure all the celebrators had left. He thought there was no one left to witness the act. But, there was one watching from above and one from below. As Kurt removed Katrina's blouse and began to mount her, the winged creature swooped down to stop him only to be met with equal force from the darkness below. Wings beat and thrashed as the battle between the light and the dark had begun. As Kurt plunged into Katrina, a sword sliced across the air between cutting his chest deep but missing his heart. An even darker blade had slashed between as well blocking the blade of light keeping his heart beating. Katrina had long passed from the world before Kurt took his liberties.

He woke the next morning feeling pain in his chest thinking Katrina had gotten off one serious blow before he took her. Quickly realizing she was dead, he called his friends at the Alliance to send someone who knew how to handle these things. The news that day would only briefly mention that a young lady was found dead at the campaign headquarters suffering from a heroin overdose. The security cameras showed she came back after everyone had left to continue the party on her own. She apparently had long suffered from drug addiction even after many attempts by the great President-Elect Kurt Buchanan to get her help. The secret service detail, Patriots all, overlooked the fact that they had all enjoyed the festivities a bit too much.

After a long nap to sleep off the alcohol, Kurt awoke and pulled out a burner phone. He placed one call to an old contact who typically only spoke with Katrina. "Roger, my old friend...yes, yes, I did try to help her as you well know, but alas she was not worth saving. It is time. Move the devices into play. Remember, there can be no trace to any of my following. Remember Los

Angeles, San Francisco, Houston, New York, Chicago, New Orleans, Seattle, Miami, and let's not forget Atlanta. And the yield is correct?"

Roger began, "Yes Sena.. I mean yes, President-Elect Buchanan, the yield is set correctly. I must caution you though even with the low yield as we all know there will be white casualties."

Kurt paused thinking about the deaths of necessity. He already appeared to be a shade near death himself when not covered in all the foundation makeup for his public showings. He scratched at the deep cut in his chest where he thought Katrina had cut him with a hidden letter opener. The wound would not heal well and oozed some grey matter. "They are Patriots, after all Roger, and know the cost for the reward of total freedom from all this pestilence. They will be rewarded. Proceed. And Roger, did not Katrina have a cousin across the way in Hazard? Yes, yes, I know, a bit taller than Katrina. I suddenly find myself in need of a new secretary at least for a bit of time." Kurt placed the phone in one of the acid bath containers Katrina had always obtained from Roger. Stupid girl, he thought, as she always assumed they were acid for his evergreen trees.

American Alliance Meeting
Washington, D.C.

The now newly elected President-Elect Buchanan, quietly stepped through the back door of the meeting hall with his secret service intact. He could not be seen publicly now attending these meetings, but his presence was necessary to continue to bolster the ranks. Antonio's continued requests for peace and reconciliation had reached a point that could not be ignored for the organization. The holy retreat center for Jesus lovers that was slowly being constructed in low

earth orbit was just another turn of the screw for
Buchanan. He could not tolerate those seen flocking to
the Holy See to distract from his movement. What he
thought was just some passing interest in praising God
and all his creation in space turned out to be a bit more
of a structured endeavor for Antonio Vieira, God's
puppet on Earth. It was time to cause Antonio to take
pause.

Kurt walked to the front amidst raucous thundering
applause. "Patriots, we have won many battles recently
in our efforts to take back America. With my election
as President, the final war has begun. We will finally
cleanse this land of all that ruin the very ideals of our
crusade for justice. The white Christian will once again
rule and we will wash the sickness from this land for all
eternity. Even now as I speak, the vessels of
righteousness are moving into place. Some of you have
expressed concerns about Antonio's activities to glorify
God's creation with his Catholic retreat in space for all

the half-breeds. This joke of a tourist attraction for followers of his petulance will not detract from our movement. We will take steps to stir the fires of our dominance. The true followers, the evangelical right wing, will prevail."

Pad 39A Cape Canaveral, Florida

There is a moment in the launch of any rocket where the beast takes on a life of its own. This night was no different except this beast was the largest rocket on the face of mother Earth. The Falcon Heavy manufactured by the SpaceX corporation sat breathing and pulsating ready to literally scream its way into space. Thrust skyward by twenty seven Merlin engines all burning a mix of refined kerosene, RP-1, and liquid oxygen, the Falcon Heavy was the only rocket capable of launching Pandere's Olympus module into space along with an extra bonus package not listed in the media publication. Roger knew that the RP-1 being used as fuel was not as combustible as the liquid hydrogen typically used by NASA. He also knew this had to look like an accident. Remembering an article written back in 2018 with some comments by Elon Musk, Roger was targeting something much simpler to pull off. While the local security force for Cape Canaveral was looking for possible drone flybys, Roger had carefully maneuvered the robot in place the night before. He was going to use SpaceX's own security robot against them. Nobody around the launch site would question why a Boston Dynamics *Spot* robot was seen wandering the facility in the off chance it was seen. Though Roger had this particular *Spot* modified to blend in with the white colors of the Falcon Heavy. Unless caught moving up the side of the rocket, it would take a keen eye indeed to detect it. There would be no radio signals as *Spot* had been programmed for this mission in advance. All *Spot* had to do was rub a few key aluminum nuts and spray them with some extra corrosive saltwater one more time. If the nuts were ever found and inspected, one would assume that somehow they were exposed to saltwater prior to launch. Roger had made certain that the powder coating designed to prevent such an occurrence had been left off by a patriot working for the forge where the special nuts were made. *Spot* had been in contact with the nuts before, but this trip was the most dangerous as there was no other activity happening around the rocket to distract motion security detectors. *Spot* slowly climbed the face of the rocket using specially designed suction cup feet and eased between the booster couplings rubbing the nuts and spraying them one last time.

When the countdown had reached the two minute mark, *Spot* had long left the rocket launch area to walk silently into the ocean where it would submerge itself to corrode away in the natural salt of the Atlantic Ocean.

As the countdown approached the ten second mark, Roger had joined the crowds in the observation area to witness his work. The announcer began over the intercom, "10, 9, 8, 7, 6, 5, 4, 3, 2, 1, main ignition, launch." The roar of the 27 merlins overwhelmed the announcer as the Falcon Heavy began to rise off the pad. At first all seemed normal, with the large plume of smoke and steam bellowing outwards from the pad slightly obscuring some very subtle motion of the core stages. Buchanan had requested the event render the launch pad useless so Roger was a bit nervous as the rocket was rising faster than he had anticipated. Not more than a thousand feet off the pad, the crowd could see that something was terribly wrong. The resonant forces of the launch had loosened the corroded nuts in place and the three core boosters began to separate. With local populations in Florida at risk of a rogue booster heading their way, SpaceX had no alternative but to perform an emergency self destruct over pad

39A. With all core boosters still mostly full of fuel and oxidizer the explosion resembled a small nuclear mushroom cloud and most of pad 39A was melted down into a pile of ruble. As one core booster had almost freed itself from the main rocket, it careened off towards the Atlantic Ocean and exploded right where *Spot* had entered the water.

Pope Vieira's private chambers Vatican City

"Monsignor Mickey, report," his Holiness practically yelled at him as he walked into his chambers. His Holiness was infuriated with the reports coming out of the United States in relation to the Falcon Heavy launch and disaster following.

Monsignor Mike began to bend down to kiss his Holiness' signet but Pope Vieira waved him off glaring at the delay. "The launch did include the Olympus module of NUERA1 your Holiness. From all reports of local media and experts in the field, the explosion was a result of some corrosion on Aluminum nuts. This happened in the past to another SpaceX launch of Falcon1, but the corporation thought all of those issues had been addressed. Perhaps since the Falcon Heavies are soon to be replaced by the Starship, quality control inspections have lapsed a bit. That is the general theme amongst the media outlets. However, we know from video feed analyzed by the Cross, that there was something peculiar moving on the rocket before launch." Monsignor Mickey passed the photo to his Holiness and spoke one word, "Sabotage."

His Holiness rose with great effort and moved to view Vatican City from his tower office window. "We knew this was expected, but it does put us behind in our final launch schedule. Thank God for our brothers and sisters in Brazil. The new launch facility will come on line shortly and it is fully protected by the Militia Sancti

Petri. The last of the Falcon 9 rockets acquired from SpaceX will be fully vetted before being fueled and launched."

"Your Holiness, things in the states are very bad as you have assumed from the media," Monsignor Mickey spoke with some hesitancy as his Holiness was already on the edge. "The patriot groups are rising up across America. It is no longer frowned upon to be a white supremacist. In some cities, they are openly and brutally beating Blacks, Hispanics, Asians...even long forgotten Native Americans are being attacked. Your Holiness, they are using His word to condone these actions. The Holy Bible is being used as a weapon once again in the land. It is almost as if the crusades have been renewed and they are attacking all that do not share and believe their words. Just yesterday the Statue of Liberty's book was vandalized and the words Holy Bible were written over July 4th, 1776."

Pope Vieira raised his hand to pause Mickey's report to ask, "How many have we lost, Mickey?" addressing him informally to calm him down. "Drop the formalities, Mickey, and give it to me like the old friends we have become. Our time is short."

Mickey paused and took a seat and spoke solemnly, "Antonio, we know of tens of thousands of casualties in the US. We are approaching over a million worldwide and growing. There have been sightings of him and the darkness so many times now that rumors are spreading the angels are descending upon us again. Are they?"

Antonio sat back down from his view of Vatican City, what was once the most respected holy place in the world. *Respected?* He frowned as the lies and the secrets ran deep. Tears were flowing down his cheeks as he realized that evil had existing in the Church for thousands of years. Millions had been killed, raped, and pillaged all in the name of Jesus as those that perpetrated those deeds read into His words what they wanted. When popes overlooked sexual child abuse amongst their own clergy, they should have known the end was coming. It was one thing to kill but yet another to damage the soul of an innocent. Thou shall not kill was a commandment,but damaging the soul of an innocent was unspoken as it was the ultimate sin, for life may end but the soul is everlasting. To damage the very soul of an individual was an affront to God Himself.

"Mickey, what I tell you now cannot be shared as it will cause panic tenfold over the losses we have now. I tell you this as my friend as our days are finished. There are others that will carry His word beyond our world only His word will change. His word has been written and misconstrued many times over the eons. The Bible is a story but many of the truths within have been twisted. Yet, many of the truths have been visible and understood by even the youngest of our tribes. So many times we chastise these innocent youth for reading what has been blatantly obvious from the Old Testament. I tell you now, Mickey, what we have always tried to hide has been revealed to me by God as truth. *As they were going along and talking, behold, there appeared a chariot of fire and horses of fire which separated the two of them. And Elijah went up by a whirlwind to heaven."* Mickey sat there frozen as a child hearing a story for the very first time from the best storyteller possible. He did not fully believe the words Pope Vieira was speaking. Somewhere deep inside he struggled with the truth. "Mickey, the chariots of fire came from outer space. As His emissaries came to bring the word of God to our world, so too shall we take the word of God beyond. NUERA1 is the vessel we will use. A chosen few will be His angels on another world."

Along the back roads of Appalachian Kentucky

To most Kentuckians that day, the three vans passing through their back country roads would have appeared like the common Amazon Prime delivery trucks seen delivering their goods. However, though these particular Ford Transit vans may have had Amazon logos painted on them, they were uniquely modified for the task at hand. Each van was reinforced with the latest armor that could deflect all light caliber ammunition, high tech military rounds, and even some light rocket propelled grenades. The Militia Sancti Petri had added modified sky lights that would fool any satellite photography tech into believing they were common vans. In reality, the sky lights could lift up revealing the Valhalla NIMROD light turrets with 30mm cannons capable of firing 1100 rounds a minute. The Vatican had these units specialized in Europe for protecting the Pope when visiting less than friendly countries. Today they would be protecting the crew of NUERA1 while visiting the back yards of the Patriots of Virginia. The

leading and trailing vans were packed with Militia
Sancti Petri armed to the teeth each with SIG Sauer
P220 pistols and SG 551 LB automatic rifles equipped
with grenade launchers. His Holiness was taking no
chances after the destruction of the Falcon Heavy. This
trip to Virginia held special importance, both for the
item they would obtain and for the lessons the crew
would learn while visiting the impoverished coal
country of Kentucky and Virginia.

Abor was taking the lead role as advisor on this trip
to Virginia. They would be obtaining the key element,
the nuclear rods, for his THOR reactor that would
power NUERA1. He was driving the lead vehicle as
only he knew the location of the secret Lightbridge
facility buried deep in the mountains of Virginia.
Lightbridge had been working with the French
company, Areva SA, to refine the use of the thorium
rods specifically for the NUERA1 nuclear drive. Abor's
design was working well in the basement of his house,

but with the special rods from Lightbridge he could improve the efficiency of his drive ten fold. Lightbridge and Areva had been working together on the EPR - Evolutionary Power Reactor, but as with all R&D projects they started with a miniature reactor using smaller rods at the test facility in Virginia. The Pope had used his contacts in France to purchase the technology and paid them some extra R&D money to even further miniaturize the rods for the NUERA1 nuclear reactor.

Abor glanced over at Jake sitting in the passenger seat thinking to himself he did not really know this person. Though he had thought he recognized him from his past, he could never quite place his finger on where. Abor spoke up "Is that really necessary on this trip?" as he glanced down at the pistol Jake had strapped on that morning. Jake was armed in a similar fashion to the Militia Sancti Petri, but he preferred the common sidearm from his pilot days, his M9 Beretta. Jake was also wearing specialized field armor as if they would be stepping out of the vans into a full on war zone.

Jake thought carefully about what he should say to Abor as he was not fully vetted in the dangers of today. "Things have changed now with destruction of our main module. As you know across America, the darkness is rising. We can no longer be blinded to the dangers that we face. His Holiness has decided it's time to face the reality that we will lose a few innocents as we prepare to launch. Of all things, we cannot afford to lose the drive. Without it, there will be no launch beyond the Earth's system. As you required the entire crew to visit the nuclear facility, we could take no chances."

Abor frowned upon the use of violence but understood full well the threats they faced. "I requested the entire crew as I cannot be the only one who understands the intricacies of the thorium reactor and drive. After all, not only will it propel us to Gliese, but it will also power the entire station. This is new technology and there may be times it might go down during the trip. If I become sick or injured, others will need to know how to restart the drive."

"Your point is well taken, Abor. As Commander of the crew, I can greatly appreciate being well educated on all facets of our ship."

Mary spoke up from the back of the van as they traversed the rough hills of Kentucky headed towards the new Cumberland Gap Tunnel leading to Virginia. "This area has not changed for decades. I cannot believe President-Elect Buchanan promised these folks a renewal of coal mining. The kids are still walking these hills barefoot with clothes that barely cover their backs. The poverty here was only slightly improved even with the mines going full force. Black lung took most of the profits from the families and fed it into the medical facilities trying to fight the disease."

Abor spoke up as his tribe knew a thing or two about promises not kept by the American government. "It has been the same across this great land of ours. We offer promises of wealth but not for those that live in the area and suffer the consequences of the environmental destruction. That wealth goes into the corporations that mine the coal and the other companies nearby that have been polluting these lands for years."

Jake, lost in memories of his past in Kentucky, joined the conversation, "Surely, Abor, you are not buying into those conspiracies about the uranium-233 storage facilities deep underground in the Cumberland Gap?"

Hayat, fighting off his jet lag coming back from a trip to Syria to collect his wife, joined in, "Jake, I am not certain about the conspiracies, but there are great places to bury and hide uranium-233 in these mountains. That book I picked up at the last stop does have some rather startling facts about the Cumberland Gap Tunnel. Over $300 million was spent to build the tunnel and bypass the historical gap area when the current road system could have just been upgraded and flattened for less than half the cost. We should never underestimate the power of uranium and the weapons it fuels. The Oakridge National Laboratory has to get rid of that waste somewhere and what better place than the backyards of people that have already been repressed and impoverished."

Coming down Wilderness Gap road, the crew of NUERA1 was not far from many of the old bustling coal towns of Kentucky, Lynch, Harlan, Middlesboro and others where the backs of many a Kentuckian were broken and the lungs of many more were poisoned. All for a fuel that could have easily been replaced by something clean if not for the darkness requiring something for ultimate death and destruction. Abor once again spoke up in defense of what he knew was the answer for a better world. "It has been said that there is more thorium on the coast of India to power city after city across the east. America has over 400,000 tons of thorium wasting away. Clean fuel with a half life of almost 14 billion years compared to the 4 billion of uranium. The radioactivity of the waste is gone in only 800 years, where as uranium is dangerously radioactive for 10,000 years. Thorium cannot be used for weapons, but it could be used to cleanly power the world without all the death and destruction from mining coal or pumping crude oil from the Earth. What we needed, He hath provided, if not for our dark ambitions to rule the world."

The van grew quiet as they approached the gap. The radio squawked as the Militia Sancti Petri called out, "Time to slow down and space out our group. We only want one van at a time going through the tunnel. It is too risky to get us all caught inside. Let us each take a pit stop in Middlesboro and depart 15 minutes apart so we each pass through the tunnel at a separate time. Safeties off, gentlemen!" Jake pulled the slide on his

Beretta to confirm a round was chambered and took off the safety. The atmosphere grew thick with tension in the vans, as they prepared to complete their passage into Virginia, and head to the mountains not far from Reston where Lightbridge kept their hidden laboratory for thorium research. Everyone knew what was at stake.

1:00 p.m.

Cumberland Gap Tunnel

The lead van had cleared the tunnel and radioed back to Abor confirming they would stop ahead and regroup after all vans had exited the tunnel. Abor had just pulled out of the gas station headed east on Hwy 25 towards the tunnel entrance. The tunnel project was a testament to the abilities of engineers to construct a four lane highway almost a mile through solid rock; two lanes east and two lanes west. Once inside the tunnel, there was no place to turn around without traffic coming to a complete stop and reversing. There were only a few areas connecting east and west bound tunnels in case an evacuation of one tunnel would be necessary. The Cumberland Gap Tunnel Authority, CGTA, employees had been experiencing intermittent power outages over the last week after the recent storms passed through. The shift supervisor, Bill Jones, had to reboot the SCADA system for the third time that morning. SCADA, short for Supervisory Control and Data Acquisition System was the control system for the security cameras, ventilation fans, smoke detectors, and linear heat detectors for the entire tunnel system. Bill never noticed that morning that one set of cameras in the cross tunnels failed to turn on. It was spring break in Kentucky and they expected well over the 24,000 cars a day they typically saw going through the tunnels as families headed to all points east and west.

Father Joe, who had been sleeping most of the trip, finally awakened with a feeling of dread. After his caving experience at Otter Creek Park during his youth, tunnels underground were not his cup of tea as they would say. At this moment, he would prefer a glass of some of that famous Tennessee whiskey to calm his nerves. Knowing he was supposed to also be the group counselor and overall spiritual advisor, he thought his time had come for a pep talk. For the moment though, he had few words coming to mind. "As we approach the entrance, let us remember the souls who lost their lives on this mountain before the tunnel was constructed. Massacre Mountain has taken many families over the years. In God's name, we pray." Not much of a speech he thought, but he was feeling more than just the weight of the mountain bearing down upon him. Joe was fighting with memories of his past, struggling to remember some connection between some members of his group and the dark soul that was ruling their country now.

Jake spoke up feeling some need to help Father Joe out a bit, "Amen, Father Joe, if memory serves, they have lost close to 400 people on the mountain since 1926 when the old road was constructed."

"Perhaps 400 mostly white folks but what about the 4000 plus Cherokee Indians that died after the white man forced them to march and leave these lands. You call this Massacre Mountain for 400 accidental traffic accidents??" Abor testily spoke up for his kind, as it weighed heavily on his heart for the last several hours thinking of what the white man had done to take these lands. As Abor drove the van through the entrance of the tunnel, tension had risen greatly inside. Jake realized that he still had a long road ahead to bring this group together for their launch. All the training leading up to this trip had still not erased thousands of years of strife. It was not lost on Jake that he was the only white man with European ancestry on the crew. Jake, lost in his thoughts about the Blacks, Muslims, and Native Americans that had been butchered by white Caucasians throughout time, missed the movement to his left as one of the cross tunnel doors opened after they passed.

Suddenly, a white flash occurred further down the tunnel in front of them and then the sound compression reached the van popping the ears of all inside. Jake and Hayat's past military training immediately kicked in driving adrenaline into their veins. Traffic had come to a sudden stop with Abor barely missing the family headed to Myrtle Beach in front of them. Jake yells, "Abor switch out," as he takes the wheel pulling out his 9mm in the process and placing in on the dash. Hayat popped the safety latch on the fake sunroof and pressed the control button to raise the NIMROD into place as the Militia Sancti Petri locked and loaded their weapons in the back of the van. Thinking their only course of action was to reverse and go back out the way they came in, Jake starts backing up to force the cars behind him to head the same way. Bad idea, he discovers, and in the rear view mirror he sees darkness filling the tunnel from behind them. Jake yells out "We are trapped folks. We have but one choice and that is forward to whatever caused that explosion." Mary reached forward and put her hand on Jake's shoulder and nodded to him, "Some innocents will be lost this day, but their souls will not be forgotten." Father Joe grabbed his cross and prayed knowing they had but little choice as they must survive to spread His word beyond. Jake threw the van forward and started pushing the beach family car out of the way as he forced the van into the middle between both lanes to negotiate their way out of the tunnel. He apologized with a glance to the father as they passed. Dread filled his heart and his soul as Jake realized the family would not survive. He said a silent prayer as they continued forward knocking one car left and one car right as the darkness continued to swell behind them. It was not just the darkness he could see, but the darkness he could feel. As if tentacles were threading around his soul, Jake knew they must escape it.

The leader of the Militia Sancti Petri yelled forward to Jake, "Stop the van for a moment and let my force depart."

Jake looked through the rear view mirror at the sergeant yelling back, "There is no way you can survive what is coming," as he could see the darkness taking shape showing its structure as wings began to show by the hundreds coming forward pouring out of the side tunnels.

The sergeant yelled back, "The unit behind has moved into the tunnel to support us. We will press the dark forces back to give you time to move forward. Sir, it is your only chance. We took an oath to Him and our lives mean nothing if we fail!" Leaving no room for argument, the sergeant opened the back and jumped out before Jake could even come to a full stop. His six man team departed immediately opening up with their SG 551 LB grenade launchers creating a hole in the pressing darkness enough to cause the winged beasts pause. Hayat swung around the NIMROD and unleashed the holy hell of war as the 30mm cannon spread death at 1100 rounds a minute. Bullets hit their mark but many ricocheted off the walls of the tunnel shredding lead and rock into bits of shrapnel, some hitting the beasts while others hit the travelers in the tunnel around them. Jake gunned the van forward fearing a glance back would reveal what he already knew; the beach family had not survived. Abor did what Jake could not and risked looking back over his shoulder. He could see the death and destruction they were leaving behind and the dreams of swimming in the Atlantic for that one family now butchered. He thought for a moment he could see a small glow rising from them. His only conciliatory thought was their souls had survived. Jake knew the team would not survive if they failed to keep moving forward and feared the force they would confront forward. Hayat sensing the same swung the NIMROD forward and prepared to once again spread death upon his fellow human beings; though he would not mind hitting a few more of those dark beasts in the process. Strange how they appeared not unlike the angel he witnessed in Syria.

Jake guessed only 1000 feet were left before they reached the end of the tunnel, but a thousand feet could take hours in a heated battle. They should have been able to see some light coming from tunnel exit. It was pitch black minus the flashes of gunfire coming from forward positions. So, Jake thought, it is not only dark beasts we face today but dark souls with more conventional weapons. "Hold on to something!" Jake screamed back as he had to ram several cars to force them out the way as the armored Amazon van held together. Jake said a silent prayer for the sergeant and his men as he knew they had paid their oath debt behind. Bringing himself to the present, Jake started to see things were looking a bit dismal forward. There were at least fifteen hard men armed to the teeth ahead with darkness surrounding them. As he began to think their faith in Him may have been misplaced, a flash of golden light shot through the tunnel as the sword was unsheathed from its scabbard. The light was almost blinding as the angel slashed through the darkness ahead.

Father Joe, of all people, lunging forward grabbed Jake's Beretta and began to yell, "For my brothers I die for thee." Father Joe's anger, tempered for years, burst forth as he unleashed round after round from Jake's 9mm. One white patriot after another could be seen jerking back as their heads exploded from the rounds. Father Joe had used the first round to shatter the windshield but each of the remaining rounds found their mark landing dead center on the foreheads of the

Patriots in the front. That left one remaining member of

the 15 squad forward which Jake dispatched with the

front end of the van. Jake, with the lapse in danger,

looked dead in Father Joe's eyes where he could see the

anger still blazing there but sadness as well. Father Joe

letting the flames of his soul cool down noticed Jake's

look and commented, "What? You think only you white

boys learned how to shoot in these here parts?" Jake

reached back and took the smoking gun from Joe's

hands and slid another magazine in place and holstered

the weapon, for a priest to take life with such disregard

had startled him. As the smoke and darkness began to

clear, Mary who had been staring out the side window

watching the one that held the blazing sword, had felt

something sharp punch her stomach. She had lost her

faith in God and angels, but swore what she had just

witnessed was real. The golden angel with wings

stretching almost the length of the van had defeated one

dark angel after another with ease. Archangel Michael she thought? But that was only stories from the Bible she had been read as a kid. It could not be real or.....as Mary reached down feeling her stomach her hand coming away wet with blood; she prayed a silent prayer *Let It Be Him*. "Gentlemen, I believe I have been hit."

Bill Jones went home to be with his family that night knowing what he witnessed could not be spoken of to them. He must protect them from the truth as they could not possibly believe his story. He had gone back to review the tapes from the security cameras. What initially had appeared as darkness and empty tunnels connecting the east and west bound lands were hordes of dark angels. He realized his error from earlier had cost many their lives. However, the words spoken to him from the angel of light dismissed all his worry. "Seek the light and you shall know the truth." The media would report almost 1000 souls had lost their lives in the tunnel that day from some toxic cloud spewing out of a truck carrying hazmat materials.

Somehow the labels on the truck showed non-toxic

materials at the checkpoint and it was allowed through.

Chapter 8

22 light-years away on Al-Ruh

Unark had been spending considerable time studying a star system far away staring intently hour upon hour every night. So much so, Tsiera was beginning to worry he may be losing touch with his flock. As Tsiera approached her father, she heard him talking to himself or it seemed perhaps he was speaking with Al-Wahid as he would sometimes do when frustrated. Though, this night her father looked sad and afraid with tears in his eyes. "Daughter, come" as he spread his arms wide to embrace her.

"Father, what is it? What is wrong?" she prodded him to see what could cause the great Unark such grief.

"Tsiera, I feel something is happening that is very sad far away in that star system. I know it is silly. How could I possibly feel anything for a star? It is not really that I feel anything for the star but when I look at that particular star, I feel the presence of Al-Wahid and it is a very sad dark feeling. Most Ruhnits only follow me because I have kept the peace in our flock. I realize many do not believe I have spoken with Al-Wahid or that the day will come when the three suns of Al-Ruh, Wahid, the life giver, and Ithnaan and Thalaatha the twins will align bringing Al-Wahid to save them from their dark deeds."

"Not I father, not I, as I have felt His presence and feel His presence daily as I connect with life on Al-Ruh."

"Yes, daughter, your gift gives you insight that others lack. But do not take it for granted as my time will soon be over and you will join with Al-Ruh to prepare the way for our forgiveness as it has been foretold. I fear though our forgiveness in the future is at risk as I gaze to the heavens. Ridiculous I know, but I feel great darkness is moving against Him." Tsiera gazed upon the star Unark had pointed out and she too felt a deep sadness. At the same time though Tsiera felt a great fierceness, a strength from within not felt before. She gazed with anger upon the star where darkness was pulling from the light. As her anger grew, so too did her fluorescence as she blazed forcefully forward into the night. "Tsiera, calm yourself....you do not yet have full control of your power. Calm your heart, my daughter, and seek the truth of the light. The light will prevail. Al-Wahid has promised darkness will be defeated on Al-Ruh. One is coming, as you know, that will need your power to fulfill the prophecy."

Lightbridge facility somewhere near Reston, Virginia

Abor had led what was left of the group of Amazon vans to the forested mountains near Reston, Virginia.

The group had taken stock of their losses and had stopped only briefly to check on Mary's wound. Lucky for her it was a through and through; no organs or bone had been hit. They had called ahead to the Lightbridge facility and there was a doctor on hand who could fix her up good as new. During the stop, they took a moment of silence to remember the near one thousand people apparently killed in the accident in the Cumberland Gap Tunnel. Abor and the rest of NUERA1's crew knew the real truth. Abor had pulled the lead van over to the side of the road as the sun was setting. Out of respect, the team was letting Hayat complete his prayers to Allah. As Hayat kneeled on his prayer rug, Jake had taken a seat at a nearby rock offering his prayers to God and asking forgiveness in his own way. Father Joe simply bowed his head staring at the ground facing the dying light of the day shaking with the sadness in his heart for the lives he had taken. Though Patriots, they were still souls, obviously lost and soon to be betrayed by their idol but souls none the less.

Mary seemed to be the most distraught of the group, though not for the shrapnel wound she had received. Having discarded her Catholic beliefs long ago for the teaching of Buddha, she was having tremendous struggles within trying to rationalize what she had seen in the tunnel. For Mary alone saw the full power and might of the Archangel Michael as he delivered blow after blow of his sword to the dark winged creatures. She refused to call them angels and refused to believe she saw the Archangel Michael. However, what the nuns had tried to teach her as a child was now in direct conflict with her spiritual beliefs and the science she worshiped as fact.

Abor called out, "It is time!" and the group filed in to the lead van with the Militia Sancti Petri giving them some distance in the second van. Abor waited to be sure there were no other cars on the road and pulled off seemingly into the ravine below where Hayat had given praise to Allah. Making a very sharp turn into what appeared to be a massive rock outcropping the van disappeared.

A representative from Lightbridge, Dr. Wilson, met them at the gate after their grand entrance into the solid rock. Jake, out of great respect for the security technology required to pull that off, spoke first, "Sir that was well done. I know a few in the US Air Force that would like to see that used at some facilities in the west."

"Yes, commander, it would take more than a few to understand how it works, but it is necessary to guard this facility and what we have worked hard to protect for his Holiness. Please accept my condolences for your losses at the tunnel. I see you are a van short plus the sergeant's group. Great losses indeed. Let us make sure they had a reason for going early to the afterlife. We will begin your tour and training on the reactor and drive immediately." Motioning a young lady forward from behind, "Dr. Harrington, I understand you sustained an injury during the attack. This is Dr. Aiko Yoshioka, our resident medical expert. She will treat your wound. Commander, Abor has assured me you all need to be up to speed on Liquid Fluoride thorium Reactors (LFTR) and the THOR drive before you leave our facility for Brazil. His Holiness wanted to relay to you, Commander, that the second Falcon Heavy launch from the facility in Brazil was successful. The Olympus module is now in orbit and autonomously transferring to final staging. Minus the unit we have here and the Nautilus modules, you are very close to completing NUERA1." This was a piece of good news the group could use as the past couple of months had been dark indeed. "Let's begin, shall we?" the representative continued as they began their tour. Jake paused to watch Mary and Dr. Yoshioka as they went to the infirmary spending a bit of extra time watching Aiko as she left. It had been a long time since such beauty had graced his presence. He felt oddly warm inside as if the Holy Spirit had just brushed his soul.

"It was his Holiness' explicit instructions that the power and propulsion module of your craft utilize something that would not contaminate your future home nor be used for mass destruction," spoke Dr. Wilson as they oversaw the final checks of the module. "We have worked long and hard on miniaturizing the technology; working both with the Russians and the French." Jake raised his eyebrows at the mention of the Russians being involved. To an old Air Force man, they were considered the enemy. Realizing they were also working on safer means of utilizing nuclear power gave him pause. Perhaps not everything he had been trained to believe about their *enemy* was true. "I will not bore you with all the intricacies of the physics, but essentially your power source is a breeder using thorium-232 which transmutes to thorium-233, briefly decaying to protactinium-233 and then decaying to uranium-233. That is where your power is going to come from; as the uranium 233 atom fissions it will generate 198MeV of energy. When this happens a thermal neutron will bombard the thorium-232 again continuing the cycle."

Hayat at this point concerned, "Dr. Wilson my nuclear physics is a bit cloudy from my days at Damascus University, but if I remember this will require us needing to obtain the highly radioactive seed material. Also this process is typically on a much larger scale than something required for a spacecraft. How are you able to..?"

Dr. Wilson interrupts, "Your physics is not that bad, Dr. Muhammad. You are correct. NUERA1 will require a small amount of uranium-233, thankfully provided by an old warhead of our Russian friends. This was necessary to conceal our efforts from the eyes of our soon to be President. Though mark my words, it will not be hidden forever. Too many eyes are watching these materials these days. Now for your reason for visiting us today, Lightbridge has been working hard testing LFTRs or lifters you can call them. We have miniaturized the thorium rods to less than a meter in our small reactors. One day we will have a reactor that will power a car using thorium. For now, we have gotten down to the size of the module you see before you." Dr. Wilson waved his hand across the view window looking into the bay where the NUERA1 power and propulsion module sat receiving its final checks before being transported to Brazil for launch aboard another Falcon Heavy. The unit was about the size of a Greyhound bus with more sophistication than reactors working in any country at that time.

As commander of NUERA1, Jake had been concerned about the safety of this reactor. Though it would not have been his first choice, it was the only choice. "Sir, could you cover again what happens during a meltdown?" Dr. Wilson began to laugh and caught himself understanding the seriousness of the question. "Jake, if I may call you that, there is no meltdown with a thorium lifter. In the bottom of the reactor there is a frozen salt plug. If there is ever any power outage or any safety alarms requiring a shutdown, the frozen plug will melt allowing the radioactive fuel to drain into a safety zone that is shielded. There is no possibility of a meltdown in this reactor. Now, let us take a look at the THOR drive that will provide propulsion for your craft." As Dr. Wilson led them down the hall to the viewing window of the next bay, Mary and Aiko rejoined the team.

Jake, thinking it was entirely too early for Mary to be up and about, spoke his concern, "Should you not be spending a bit more time in the infirmary, Mary?"

Aiko spoke up, "Actually, her wound only required a few stitches and we gave her an entire bag of saline with antibiotics."

"It is ok Jak... I mean Commander, I feel as strong as a horse now," Mary spoke up for herself a bit red in the cheek at all the concern. Physically Mary did feel fine,but on a deeper level there was a battle waging inside her. She was a scientist not easily swayed by theatrics or even something someone might see with their own eyes. As the lead astrophysicist and navigator for NUERA1, should she mention what she thought she saw in the tunnel? It did not appear that anyone else was openly discussing the event other than the loss of some members of the Militia Sancti Petri. Surely Hayat was not just randomly firing the NIMROD at darkness without seeing his targets. Well there were flashes of light, presumably muzzle fire coming from that direction so perhaps he did not see. Jake noticed Mary was not being totally truthful about her condition. He thought that through all the training he should know his team better. It was one thing to prove yourself in battle or a military training exercise and develop camaraderie amongst the troops. Jake was learning it was a far different thing to bring together a group of scientists to work together as a team where you knew everyone had your back.

"Your THOR drive will have the specific impulse of almost twice previous nuclear powered propulsion systems developed in the past by the US and the Russians. With some special modifications you will be pushing 1200 seconds. Your drive will be uniquely tied to the reactor utilizing the thorium-228 waste byproduct. The decay heat of thorium-228 will be used to super heat hydrogen gas upwards of 3400K which propelled out the nozzle of your drive provides your thrust."

"There is a whole universe of hydrogen out there of course, Dr. Wilson, but we are taking a long trip. How do we expect to launch enough hydrogen?" Mary, putting aside her experience in the tunnel, was beginning to concentrate more on the matter at hand.

"You are correct, Mary, you will need large amounts of hydrogen, some of which will be launched with the different components of NUERA1 bound up in the water that will serve as your shielding. However, Hayat Muhammad's Environmental Control and Life Support System that will be used for NUERA1 is going to also provide hydrogen from your biological waste. As I am sure you are very aware, the methane molecule is one atom carbon and four atoms of hydrogen."

"I will be using a special bacterial developed by my friend, S. Venkata Mohan, to convert all of our waste into useful components. One of which is a steady stream of hydrogen for our THOR drive." Hayat appreciated the concern of his fellow crew members, as he knew most of them were not used to living off the land so to speak. In Syria, India, and many other countries in the world, people were not as gluttonous as the capitalistic societies of the world. "We cannot stop to smell the flowers along the way and pick up extra supplies. I hope by now everyone realizes we must take everything with us and waste nothing," spoke Hayat with a bit of humor to lighten the mood.

From the back of the group, Father Joe spoke up shaking off his sins against God, "From dust you were born and to dust you shall return."

Hayat catching his thought, "Yes Joe, even our very bodies will need to be used along the way to fertilize the plants that will sustain us. Remember we are also 98% water. We cannot waste anything. We must *Pay the Dirt*." At once they all remembered the words of Pope Vieira: *This is a Generation Ship*. They all knew what that meant, but it was now sinking in and there was zero doubt. Their children would have to complete the mission.

Voicing what was on all of their minds, Dr Wilson stepped forward, "Yes, crew of NUERA1, as his Holiness I know mentioned to you in the past, but perhaps not in these specific words you will all die on board NUERA1. The THOR drive has a low thrust and your speed will continue to build as you progress but even with the optimized efficiencies we have built in, NUERA1 will take at least 126 years to reach her destination. You see at some point you have to turn the engines around and reverse thrust to slow down enough to be captured by the gravity of Gliese 667Cc. We do not have enough data on the Gliese system to utilize any other gravity wells to slow you down without significant risk."

"Count it all joy, my brothers, when you meet trials of various kinds, for you know that the testing of your faith produces steadfastness," spoke Father Joe and Hayat finished for him, "And know that your possessions and your children are a test, and that with Allah is immense reward."

Jake, understanding the gravity of the moment and how his team was growing together, pulled Dr. Wilson aside for a quiet discussion. "Dr. Wilson, I understand his Holiness' request to utilize thorium. I even appreciate the value of a high specific impulse. However, as a pilot there is...how shall I say this without sounding *TopGun*...at times there is *the need for speed*."

"Oh yes Commander, I am fully aware that you are going into the unknown here. Each individual module of NUERA1 has a conventional propulsion system for high thrust and maneuvering. The Command Control Communications module will allow you to access all units together. I caution you though this should only be activated in case of an extreme situation. Do not forget your basic Newtonian physics...for every action there is a reaction."

"Yes Sir," Jake frowned as memories of his ejection from his jet over Syria brought back vivid memories of Newton's laws. Turning back to the crew, "Folks, let us wrap this up for today. Starting tomorrow we have a solid month here of learning these systems and working with the simulators so we can learn to operate and live

upon NUERA1."

Chapter 9

In the year of our Lord 2025

Alcântara Launch Facility, State of Maranhão, Brazil

"Five, four, three, two, engine ignition, and launch." announced the intercom as two mighty Delta IV rockets manufactured by the United Launch Alliance (ULA) rose from twin pads at the same time. A first for ULA as any launch was risky, but lighting two rockets at the same time was a very delicate complex operation indeed. Pope Vieira was not taking any chances after the loss of the Falcon Heavy last year. The might of the Catholic Church in Brazil was a dim twilight now with evangelicals at almost 50% of the population. However, there were still staunch supporters of Pope Vieira in the country that could be trusted. Calling on favors too many to count, Pope Vieira arranged for the Nautilus gravity modules to launch from Alcântara. Launching the twin Nautilus modules from Alcântara's location nearly on the equator would save a great amount of money. The isolated location was also easily fortified and protected by the Militia Sancti Petri. The modules would aim for a geostationary orbit easily achieved by an equatorial launch. At least, that was the suggested final destination. If any government was monitoring the launch, it would appear Brazil was launching some massive communication satellites and most would move on to other more interesting activities. The timing of the launch was not coincidentally the same as the launch of the NASA astronauts to the Gateway facility in lunar orbit. All eyes of the media would be watching the Artemis IV launch in Cape Canaveral. The American Alliances' destruction of the Falcon Heavy under the shadowy direction of now President Buchanan had dealt a major blow to the Christian retreat center being constructed in space. Most churches were now directing their members to reconsider sending any delegations to visit the structure for the foreseeable future. The thought was to wait for SpaceX's Starships soon to be commissioned and approved by the FAA for public flights. The Falcon series of rockets from SpaceX were reaching the end of their life cycle and would soon be replaced by the more economical Starship platform. Pope Vieira had directed Monsignor Mike to take advantage of this and purchase enough Falcon 9s to launch the crew and passengers of NUERA1 from the facility at Alcântara and other locations around the world.

Somewhere in the Amazon Jungle, Mato Grosso region of Brazil

"I am sure it is this way," focusing on his compass as he walked, Jake almost plowed right over Aiko Yoshioka who had stopped to take a closer look at one of the regions more unusual lizards. The team had been experiencing issues all morning with GPS and even Jake's normally reliable compass. It had been several months since the disaster in the Cumberland tunnel. Jake had made a point of forcing the team to concentrate on the future and let the past stay in the past. As it turned out, finding Mary medical help from Aiko Yoshioka at Lightbridge was not by accident. Pope Vieira's team overseeing the crew and passenger selection for NUERA1 realized the importance of adding to their medical staff. Dr. Aiko Yoshioka trained in general primary care also specialized in prenatal care and even did a research project on radiation exposure during the Fukushima Daiichi nuclear disaster. Jake knew that even though the thorium drive was ten times safer than uranium, they still had to contend with radiation from the uranium-233 seed material and the spent thorium reactor rods. He was happy to have her on the team. Their trip through the Amazon jungle served two purposes; it was a physical fitness training exercise to get the crew in their absolute best shape before launch and a recruitment trip to obtain one more crew member. As commander of NUERA1, Jake had to consider all risks and taking on a crew member only a few months before launch seemed a very big risk. He needed his crew acting together as one in any emergency. It would be difficult at best to mold another member into the crew at this point. His Holiness, Antonio had pressed upon him the importance of this final member. They needed a very diverse genetic gene pool and her rather unique talents.

The jungle around the crew had quieted considerably in the past few minutes. Though there were members of the Militia Sancti Petri nearby, the team grew a bit anxious without them physically being on site. They would have to rely on Jake and Hayat's quick reflexes from their military training and their side arms in case they were attacked. The group began to whisper as they all realized something was not right. Mary and Father Joe turned to see if Jake and Hayat were prepared, but they already had pulled their side arms ready to unload on some attacker, man or beast. SMACK, Father Joe slaps his hand against his cheek swearing, "Jesus!" as the blood of a mosquito the size of a large Kentucky horse fly dripped down his cheek. Everyone had turned to see the commotion and swearing of Father Joe.

As if part of the very jungle itself, the leaves parted behind the crew and she appears "Olá, Amigas and Amigos! Como você está?"

Mary yells out, "Sweet Mary and Joseph, you scared us. You should not jump folks like that!" Mary's hands were shaking uncontrollably as she quickly placed them behind her back. Not before Jake noticed and made a mental note to address this later. Jake, recognizing the beautiful bronze young lady before him, reached over and lowered Hayat's weapon.

"Normally those mosquitoes go after the homem-branco down here. I would recommend you not wear so much deodorant ah...Father Joe is it? as they would not bother your beautiful ebony self with all the sweet branco blood around. Ms. Andreia Almeirão Santos in the flesh. By the way, you may have missed the latest weather report on your trip but compasses and GPS units will not work well here. The South Atlantic Anomaly has been increasing in size and possibly splitting in two. All those particles from the Van Allen Radiation belt are bouncing around down here on occasion wrecking havoc with navigation."

Jake gave Ms. Santos a frown, "You have been following us that far back? You know we could have shot you. Crew of NUERA1, where Hayat is our waste disposal expert, Dr. Andreia Santos here is our gardener. From what his Holiness tells me, she can grow anything. Meet NUERA1's Bioregenerative Life Support Systems expert. Now, Andreia, do you want to tell me why we had to dig you up all the way out here?"

"As you know the Kuikúro tribe has been linked recently to a pre-Columbian civilization right here in the area you have been hiking. On one of the pieces of pottery discovered there is a sketch of a snake plant, Sansevieria trifasciata zeylanica, to be exact. Yes, I know, not all that interesting by itself. You Yankees call them Mother-In-Law plants because you cannot get rid of them. They are hard to kill. What makes this sketch unique is the fact that this Snake Plant is drawn with fruit. Snake plants are super for several reasons. Most important, they produce large amounts of oxygen during the day but also at night. Your NASA has also shown that these plants can cleanse the air removing contaminants like formaldehyde, nitrogen oxide, xylene, benzene, and trichloroethylene and probably a host of other things not yet tested. To find one that grows fruit is a tremendous asset for our mission." The entire crew understanding the importance of oxygen and another food source waited impatiently to learn if this plant was found.

Hayat spoke up first, "And did you find this elusive specimen?"

"I did indeed and numerous fruit as well with which we can seed our future garden."

Aiko concerned with bringing aboard something only recently discovered expressed her concern, "Ms. Andreia Santos, there is a great risk that this new specimen could contain toxins and therefore poisonous on some level. How do we know for certain...,"

Before she could finish Andreia had whipped out a piece of the fruit and sucked on it with her full lips already stained by the fruit. "Well, I sort of had to test this myself over the last few days," winking out of the corner of her eye at Jake. Aiko's concern was warranted, but Jake had already received a full analysis on the plant from the lab in Rio de Janeiro. Andreia had

a sample flown out of the nearby airfield at Cuicuru.

Not only was the fruit safe to eat, it was packed full of

antioxidants. The lab also noted it required very little

water.

West Wing of the White House, Washington, D.C.

President Kurt Buchanan had just finished his state of

the union address with thunderous applause from the

Republicans. His plans to stop all immigration into the

United States except from very specific European

countries were received with wild praise from the

conservative right wing. Just a month back, he had

achieved a conservative majority on the court

promising the end of Roe V. Wade. It was purely a

numbers game that was being played out between the

darkness and the light. On one end, yes technically, if

Roe V. Wade was overturned, the new law would bring more babies into the world. On the other, many of the babies would be born into poverty and Buchanan was assured they would become addicted to the white god and sell their souls for more. The darkness was going to rape the land of its souls and poison the very creation of God along the way. President Buchanan would be using the very greed of the conservative, white right wing to pollute the land with his environmental policies. He knew there would be resistance, but the devices would solve two problems. He would rid the country of the minorities while providing an irrefutable reason for establishing martial law. Once that happened, the Patriots would achieve total control. After the freedom of the US was squashed, they would move to take the world next. A light wrap on the hidden door to the West Wing, broke his thoughts, "Sir, your guest has arrived." Having Patriots in the secret service had proven very useful. Though he was forced to remarry his wife for appearances as the country demanded a First Lady, he could still have his fun.

Laura stumbled a bit as she entered the room with the shakes of needing another fix. Kurt smiled as he realized she favored another vivacious blonde actress that a Catholic had brought through the back door numerous times into the White House. How his former predecessor had pulled that off under the nose of the Church should not have been a surprise to him. After all, celibacy amongst the clergy was simply a ruse to convince the flock of their moral superiority. Less than 50% of the priests even attempted celibacy and from the abuse of the faithful over time, there were thousands upon thousands of people walking the Earth thanks to a priest. The Church only cared that one of their own was in the White House at the time. Kurt's smile broadened even further as he thought how the mighty Catholic Church had fallen and how the Evangelical Church was spreading their word and their power now. Excited to sample Laura's forbidden fruit, Kurt sighed as business must come first. Laura also had concealed in her bosom a burn phone for talking with the Alliance. The phone ringing insatiably required his attention. "Pass it over, love." As Laura pulled out the phone, Kurt could see she had no bra and was barely covering herself in her dress. Little did he know the caller was about to ruin his mood.

"Roger, I had expected to hear from you hours ago. You are wasting my valuable time here this evening."

Roger Clanton, the American Alliance's covert operations leader, knew to choose his next few words carefully. "Sir, as planned, the X-37B had maneuvered the satellite into place and it was programmed to deburn and reenter the atmosphere over the Mato Grosso region of Brazil. The NUERA1 crew was being tracked and the satellite should have burned through the atmosphere raining the radioactive plutonium down on their exact location."

Best laid plans was all Kurt could think as he watched Laura undressing; his mood soured further. He knew Roger was about to ruin the rest of his evening.

"Sir, the X-37B should have left the region, but communications with the craft went down. It appears our man in the US Space Force underestimated the expansion of the South Atlantic Anomaly."

"Spit it out, Roger, am I going to be watching something on the morning news?" at this point President Buchanan was furious as he had apparently promoted and put his faith in the wrong man in the US Space Force..

"Sir, you should turn on Fox News." Roger hung up the phone not wanting to feel the wrath of President Buchanan. Swearing, at times, he could feel the darkness through the phone even thousands of miles away.

Kurt's dark thoughts turned his grey skin even darker as he turned on the news channel. "Reports out of Rio de Janeiro are sketchy at this time. We do not yet have video on the ground. It appears a US X-37B, and a satellite of unknown origin, have burned up through the atmosphere. Fires are raging in the favella. It is unconfirmed, but an anonymous source says radiation levels are hampering efforts to stop the flames. Firefighters cannot get close to stop the raging wall of radioactive flames moving through the favella....my God....please!" The Fox News announcer from Rio de Janeiro, in tears, could not continue speaking shaking and sobbing with horror as she realized over 1.5 million Brazilians lived in the favellas, slums of Rio. President Buchanan turned off the remote smiling and laughing even though his plans had been altered. Pausing only briefly to send a text to his chief of staff; *Make preparations to greet the crew of* NUERA1 *before launch*. They may have missed taking out the crew of Antonio's Christian lifeboat, but how fortuitous to clean so many more of his pestulant followers from Brazil.

Amazon Jungle, Mato Grosso region of Brazil

Jake put down the radio, white as a ghost, and gathered the crew bringing Andreia close to whisper something in her ear. Andreia Almeirão Santos, with a fire blazing in her eyes, screamed a blood curdling scream true to the warrior in her blood. She began to sing the song of the Jamurikumál calling on the strength of the spirits of all women of her tribe's past. Jake quietly addressing the rest of the crew, "Rio de Janeiro is burning. The fires are radioactive and cannot be stopped. Estimates are thousands will die. The Vatican reports sightings of a US Space Force logo on the wreckage that rained down causing the fires. Pope Vieira himself has requested we move up the launch date. Folks, the crew of NUERA1 will launch three weeks from today on April 21, Tiradentes Day. We need to double time it to the airfield in Cuicuru where the Militia Sancti Petri will fly us direct to São Luís. We will then take a boat over to the coast near Alcântara. I have pushed you all hard here in the jungle. If possible we will take a day to unwind, and then it is all work until launch."

Abor pushed forward through the group to ask Jake a question. Jake already could guess his concern, "Abor and Hayat, your families are being airlifted shortly to meet up with us in Alcântara."

As one, they breathed a sigh of relief, "Thank you Sir."

10:00 p.m. April 3rd, Sunday, 18 days before launch
The Cathedral of São Luís

The tension was extremely high in the crew. The flight from the dirt airfield at Cuicuru had been rough as the plane sent at the last moment to grab the crew was overloaded. It was not just the flight though. The crew had been in the jungle for weeks training. The news of the near miss on their group and the loss of life in Rio de Janiero was tasking everyone's nerves. Abor and Hayat were concerned about their families being rushed to join them. Father Joe was still deeply distraught over taking those lives in the Cumberland Gap. Mary was suffering from sights as of yet unspoken to the group as a whole. Jake could see the signs of mental fatigue throughout the group. They were in peak physical shape, but mentally they needed some down time. It was Father Joe who mentioned the Cathedral as a place to seek some peace before they crossed over to Alcantara. The group was mixed with respect to their various religions, but there was something quieting about a spiritual gathering place. They were just very peaceful, safe places to pay one's respect to the Supreme Being no matter what name given.

The cathedral was empty at this time of night and only dimly lit by candles. Decorations were already in place for the Tiradentes Day celebration where they would have a mass celebrating the dentist who organized the rebellion against the Portuguese. Eventually his rebellion lead to Brazil's liberation. Father Joe led the way into the main chapel explaining the celebration and the role of the Catholic Church in Brazil. "At the point the Portuguese were about to be overrun by the French, the soldiers prayed, and our Lady of Victory saved them. In 1619, the first original church built in honor of our Blessed Mother was constructed by 3rd Captain-General Diogo Machado da Costa." Jake noticed his crew taking in the cathedral respectively keeping their voices low in reverence. A sense of calm was growing over the crew and almost everyone was beginning to relax.

Mary, however, was beginning to shake uncontrollably and could no longer hide the fact behind her back. The paintings and especially the dark, sky blue, dome above the main altar depicting twenty-four angels was beginning to unravel Mary. At her breaking point, Mary yelled out, "Stop, enough of this! Are we not ever going to discuss what happened in the Cumberland Gap Tunnel? Surely to God, I am not the only one who saw....the shapes in the darkness." Struggling to even describe what she had seen, Mary pointed up at the dome. "I can assure you they were not smiling pale face creatures as depicted there. They were dark and evil...except for the one." Jake and Hayat exchanged a glance remembering something from Syria they were never to discuss again. Jake realized his error now in not having each crew member evaluated after the incident. Here they were eighteen days from launch and at least one of the crew was showing clear signs of PTSD. Jake reached over to place his arm on Mary's shoulder which she quickly shrugged off. "I am not going to be coddled. I know what I saw. I am not going crazy." As if on queue, the ceiling painting that had disturbed Mary began to brighten.

The Lady of Victory portrayed in the center of the painting began to brighten considerably and the angels surrounding her appeared to shift. The Lady of Victory or the Blessed Virgin Mary, for whom Mary Harrington was named spoke, "Yes, I can assure, Dr. Mary Harrington, you are very much sane." The image of the Lady of Victory began to brighten further and transformed into the most beautiful creature ever imagined. Battle hardened by millennia of battles, Archangel Michael flew down from the ceiling and rested near the altar before them. "Jake, Hayat, glad to see you are still following the truth and the light." Beginning to stumble to their knees in praise, Michael grabbed them both by the shoulders and raised them back up.

"I think perhaps the time has come to reveal to you all, the truth behind the light. Mary forgive me for the

violence you witnessed in the tunnel. You are correct.
There were shapes in the darkness. Perhaps we should
all sit down as this will come as a surprise to all of you.
Our time is short so I must get to the point quickly. My
race has been on your planet for thousands of years
serving Him. Your Bible has some things correct," as
he glanced towards Father Joe and Jake "and the Koran
as well" with a nod towards Hayat. "But, many things
have been mistranslated over the years, and many more
misconstrued. What you call angels is my race,
the....well there is not really a translation in any of your
languages, but let us just say Yahwehians. We are a
race of winged humanoids that serve Him and have for
millennia. You have depicted us on reliefs, ancient
pictographs, and rock paintings across your world.
Your Tell Halaf in Syria, Hayat, pictographs in Utah
left by your ancestors, Abor, to the Angels of Ek'
Balam in the Yucatan peninsula, or even the rock
paintings your people discovered in the rain forest of

Columbia not far from here, Andreia. Yes, Aiko, even in the Empire of Japan you have portrayed my race as *Tennin.* Like all races, we are capable of great wondrous deeds, but sadly some of my kind are also driven by darkness. Mary, you witnessed me having to put an end to some of that darkness."

"My race has visited this planet on *Wings of Chariots* as you say in your Bible. Rocket ships would not necessarily define them, but it is close enough. Our technology is far different than yours. I say we serve Him but only to try to work within the confines of your understanding. Our God is not a Him, a Her, or any other word you are capable of understanding. For simplicity sake, I will use Him to describe God so we have some common ground. Know that your mission is one that has been duplicated thousands of times across galaxies of His creation. It is one of balance to spread light where darkness is trying to overcome. Each of you as part of the crew of NUERA1 has been chosen for you particular talents but also for your genetic background. We also chose each of you for your unshakable belief in the spirit within all of us. You all of course define this differently, but still, it is there. You will be called upon many times to pull strength from the spirit on your voyage." Archangel Michael paused at this point knowing this was probably too much for them to take all at once.

"You expect us to believe that you are some Archangel of God on a mission to spread light throughout the galaxy," Mary had calmed quite a bit as Michael was speaking, though her sensibilities as a scientist could no longer hold her tongue. "And you expect us to continue your mission on another planet? Ha, I went along with this charade from the beginning because I could see this voyage of the Vatican's as the only way for me to explore beyond this world. And it just so happened, the destination was the very set of planets I had been studying. The research, of course, your Holiness decided to cover up. You cannot expect me to believe all this mumbo jumbo about angels, and missions."

Mary had been holding tight to the necklace of Buddha around her neck as she chided Michael. Besides her belief in science, her belief in the spirit was the only thing that kept her grounded all these years. After the loss of her child, and then her divorce, it had taken years before she believed in anything again. It was only on a trip to Aiko's country of Japan for an astrophysics convention did she find God again. Not in the way Christians would support but in a way she could. Mary had been struggling trying to find support for her studies and grants were fading away. At the Zenkō-ji Temple in Nagano, she felt His presence, the calming spirit that rooted her again to the Earth. She forgave herself for the past and the healing began.

"Kami no ibuki....the breath of God. We know about your visit to the temple at Nagano, Mary. I know this can all seem fantastical. As a scientist though, you can see the truth has always been there. The evidence is overwhelming across your world that you have been visited numerous times for thousands upon thousands of years. Is our existence so hard to believe? We are tasked with keeping balance. This world is out of balance and a reckoning is coming. Before that can take place, we will send the best of your kind to spread the light to yet another world. It has been this way since the beginning."

With a nod to Jake, Archangel Michael rose to stand, "I realize your time is short with only days before launch. You will not return to this world. It would not be the same if you did. Trust in Him that we have put together the most technologically advanced spacecraft from your planet for your voyage. It will not be easy, but He will be with you. The spirit within you will stay strong. To ward off the darkness, He has allowed me to provide you with a gift." Archangel Michael reached behind him and pulled an extra sword and sheath from his back. "This can only be used by the strongest in spirit amongst you and only in times of greatest peril. Your conventional weapons are not safe on the spacecraft as you may imagine." Michael placed the sword into Jake's hands, "May Yahweh guard your soul and the souls of NUERA1." At that, the Yahwehian, the great Archangel Michael, warrior for God, spread his wings and flew to the ceiling of the chapel vanishing into the night.

Chapter 10

8:00 a.m. Monday, April 5th

Rio de Janeiro, Brazil

"Jake Young, a Catholic and former US Air Force pilot will be the pilot and commander of NUERA1. Abornazine Jones, a member of the Abenaki Indian tribe, will be Chief Engineer, Dr. Hayat Muhammad, a Muslim, and graduate from Syria's Damascus University, will be Chief Life Support Officer, Dr. Aiko Yoshioka, from the island of Japan, will be Chief Medical Officer, Dr. Andreia Santos, direct descendent of the lost civilizations of the Amazon region known as Mato Grosso and member of the Kuikúro tribe, will be Chief Astrobotanist, Dr. Mary Harrington, a Buddhist and astrophysicist, will be the Chief Navigator, and last but not least Dr. Joe Washington, Father Joe, Catholic priest and psychologist, will be Chief Counselor." The reporter Larry Dawson had named off the officers of Pope Vieira's retreat in space ready for the volley of questions that he would fire at Pope Vieira.

His Holiness representing a long line of popes for the Catholic Church was well trained in subterfuge. For thousands of years the Holy See had kept many secrets revealing only partial truths to quell unrest and to align the masses with the teachings of the Church. He knew it would be necessary to reveal just enough facts about the crew to support the foundation of the retreat center without giving away the true mission. "Your Holiness, if I may begin, this is a rather unusual set of officers for a Christian retreat center in low earth orbit. One could ask what purpose does an orbiting space retreat need with an astrobotanist or an astrophysicist for that matter."

Pope Vieira spoke very eloquently and politely to Mr. Dawson, "Larry, if I may, our retreat center is aiming to be self sufficient in all aspects. As you know, these are dark times indeed on the Earth. We have lost our way and darkness is spreading in the hearts of humankind. The very soul of your great United States is dying. Forgive me, but even the media has lost her way in this world. Our retreat center will be a new guiding light. A place where those who are losing faith can come to see the gift He has given us; the fragile Earth below. We will study the very life he has given to sustain our bodies. We will meditate deeply on the life below us and the life that may exist out there in His universe. My hope is those that visit will return to Earth with a renewed hope in our existence."

Showing his utter lack of respect for his Holiness, Larry slips, "Vieira, ah, excuse me I mean your Holiness, Pope Vieira, you have to agree that America is still the greatest country on Earth. We are a beacon of light and an example to all of how to lead the world and our people."

"Larry, America is starving His children and turning away those less fortunate. I would ask your listeners, where is the light in that? The mighty power of the American Space Force destroying the favella of Rio de Janiero is a beacon of light??"

"Sir, that was ruled as an accident by the FAA, the US and Brazilian Air Forces. It was determined the cause of the reentry was related to the South Atlantic Anomaly fluctuations seen recently." Larry was doing his job and getting under the skin of Pope Vieira, "Larry, you must know by now that the X-37B was viewed by Brazilian Air Force jets coming through the atmosphere apparently still docked with the satellite. Surely this must give you some pause and ask the question as to why a US Space Force operation was taking place over Brazil during these South Atlantic Anomaly fluctuations."

Pope Vieira felt immense guilt, though having nothing to do with the disaster in Rio de Janeiro; the

Vatican did use the radiation as cover for sneaking into Brazil the seed material uranium-233 for NUERA1's reactor. Flustered but realizing this interview was getting off track, his Holiness tried to turn the tone of the interview back to one of prayer and reconciliation. "Larry, history will show the truth long after you and I are gone. At this time, we must pray for the lost souls of the Rio de Janeiro favella and hope and pray for the survivors of this tragedy. It is my hope and the hope of the Church, that the NUERA1 retreat center will be a beacon for all faiths of God to find a common belief of His word to bind us together. We live on one world Mother Earth. We are all His children no matter faith, creed, race, or color."

Larry seeing their time was up, "Well there you have it folks, NUERA1, your faith booster in space launching April 24th. Many thanks for Vieira, ah-hem, Pope Vieira for taking time out of his schedule visiting and praying for the residents of Rio de Janeiro to discuss the Holy See's LEO space retreat". As Pope Vieira left the studio, he could not help but smile, as the actual launch date was still a well kept secret.

5:00 p.m., April 7th

Ribeirinhos Club near Alcântara Launch Facility

Jake had arranged for one day of family time with the crew at a local swim club called Ribeirinhos. Tomorrow they would all be in quarantine for the final 14 days before launch to protect them against any viruses they could come in contact with on Earth. He smiled as he watched Abor's son, Mark Leo, yelling "Cannonball" as he jumped from the side of the pool. Abor's wife and son had joined them as well as Hayat's wife, but they would launch separately a week later. Jake's smile faded as he realized they would have to meet remotely with President Buchanan later this evening. He struggled to understand his trepidation with meeting with Buchanan. He knew memories of his childhood were distant and some unreachable from his experiences with his 5th grade teacher. He just could not seem to put his finger on the dark thoughts he had when his former senator of Kentucky was mentioned. Jake tried to put his dark thoughts aside as he called the main crew over for a quick meeting.

"As you know this evening we have a quick sound bite with the President of the United States to discuss our *retreat.* You have all previously been briefed on what to say about our retreat. Remember your training, folks. It is of the utmost importance that nobody knows the real mission." Jake made eye contact with each member of the crew receiving nodes all around. Everyone understood the importance of the mission. Perhaps some were struggling with their perception of the real universe after meeting with Archangel Michael. They all believed in the mission and were committed.

They all believed in Commander Jake Young and would follow him to the end. This evening Commander Young was all business. "Starting tomorrow we will all spend time each day in the tank simulator for some final training to refamiliarize ourselves with the ship. Doctors, Harrington, Hayat, and Jones will go over the intricacies of our key systems again. I expect everyone to spend time in the greenhouse with Dr. Santos. Our very lives depend on all of us having green thumbs. Dr. Washington is going to interview each of us again to ensure mission readiness and everyone will meet with Dr. Yoshioka for a final physical. Andreia looked around at the group with a sly smile, "We are the seven Amigos, no? The Magnificient Seven?" As one they toasted, "To the Magnificient Seven." Even Jake could appreciate having some comic relief and the group was bonding well together like those *Amigos* in that old western movie. He just hoped some of them would not die along the way before reaching a ripe old age.

7:00 p.m.

Communication Room Alcântara Launch Facility

The control operator signaled, "Going live in 3, 2, 1."

Jake Young spoke first to introduce himself, "Mr. President, we are honored to speak with you today about our upcoming launch to the Catholic retreat center, NUERA1. Allow me to introduce, Dr. Abornazine Jones, Dr. Aiko Yoshioka, Dr. Mary Harrington, Dr. Hayat Muhammad, Dr. Andreia Santos, and Dr. Joe Washington" As Jake was introducing the members of the crew, the video conference camera at Camp David, where President Buchanan was receiving their call, zoomed in on President Buchanan only showing his face. Jake continued to describe the flight up to the orbiting retreat station and how they would setup the center and invite various groups for retreats.

Something was wrong with Jake as he was sweating profusely. Oddly enough Joe and Abor were also sweating profusely and each seemed very agitated. Joe could not sit and began to pace behind Jake. Abor had begun to bounce his leg somewhat violently just outside of the camera view. Aiko and Mary tried to calm the men as President Buchanan began to speak, "I am proud of what our country has established in space. If it were not for the commercial space program, Antonio's I mean Pope Vieira's retreat center would not be possible." President Buchanan had realized just a moment before, when the crew was being introduced, where he knew Father Joe from. He also remembered Abor and Jake. "You boys have come a long way since we met at altar boy training at St. Katherine's Church. Heck, I have come a long way since then as well. Remember the *special* training we received to greet Pope Bessarion? Ah, you were some fine specimens, and have grown up, I see, to be fine men representing our state of Kentucky."

A sick grin spread across the face of President Buchanan as he dug even deeper as if plunging a fire poker into the men, "Heck, Joe, I cannot be prouder of you as the only black boy in the group at the time. Back in those days, you were our poster boy for acceptance of black folk into the Church. About time I said, about time." Luckily, the camera lights were still red in Alcântara, as Jake, Abor, and Joe were not well. The memories long suppressed were flooding back from that day. Kurt being the oldest and most experienced of the altar boys had been given special privileges to train the younger boys. The Church, like they did with priests, turned a blind eye to some protests by parishioners during that period. Kurt's parents were fine upstanding members of the Church and donated heavily to the coffers. Kurt was a straight A student and a wonderful representation of a fine young Catholic man.

Father Clanton ignored the protests and continued to allow Kurt to supervise the new initiates. "I hope you remember your training well, men." Kurt fondly remembered his initiation training as he forced each young boy to strip for inspection as he felt each boy's privates. As he thought, "I mean you have to measure up to be an altar boy. We cannot have any little boys here." Jake had turned a pale white and became sick to himself as Joe and Abor had already left the room with Mary and Aiko following quickly behind. Quickly checking that the cameras on their end were still off, Jake signaled moving his hand across his neck to the control operator to cut the feed. Only Hayat and Andreia remained and the expressions on their faces spoke volumes. The fires of righteousness had been stoked today. If anyone had any doubts about their mission, they had been erased.

7:30 p.m.

Washington, DC

President Buchanan knew the comm controller in Brazil was just making excuses. There were no real communication issues. The team just did not want to talk to old Kurt, captain of St. Katherine's altar boys. Quickly placing a call to Roger Clanton, he knew now that something was very wrong with this retreat in space. "Roger, we need to double our efforts to get a man to this retreat center of Antonio's. I hope you have not forgotten the aid given to you when you lost your parish. Our fun and games so many years ago may be coming back to see the light of day. Remember, I helped bury all the evidence so your name was not completely ruined. It is payback time, Father Clanton." Though President Buchanan could not see Roger, if he could, he would have seen the man red as blood with shame but mad with fury. "Kurt, your sins of the flesh have not been forgotten either! Keep that in mind!" President Buchanan hung up the phone thinking that perhaps good ole Father Roger Clanton may soon become a liability to the alliance.

22 light-years away on Al-Ruh

"We lost five more today, father. Their deaths were just as bloody as the last." Tsiera spoke softly to her father as he lay sick in bed.

The great Unark struggled to sit up as he spoke his last words. "It is the darkness spreading as it was foretold to me by Al-Wahid my daughter. Ruhnits have forgotten Al-Wahid and have forgotten the promise we keep to all life on Al-Ruh. The scales are tipping and I see us spilling into the void of Thaqab 'Aswad - the black hole of death. Tsiera, abnataya alhabiba, my beloved daughter, my time has come to an end."

"No Father, no, you are still the strongest of all on Al-Ruh," Tsiera distraught grabbed and squeezed her father's hand.

"Tsiera, now, now, it is ok, help your old father over to the window." Tsiera gathered her father and carried him to the window which only weeks ago would not have been possible. He had lost too much weight with the sickness. His light was fading too fast for Tsiera to compensate with her own energy.

"Tsiera, this will be my last arc of Wahid and your final lesson from the great Unark." As he winked at Tsiera, tears of blue fluorescence flowed down her cheeks. Wiping the tears away, Unark pulled Tsiera's hands into the rays of Al-Wahid. He began, "Feel Wahid's dying rays, feel the heat, the everlasting life. This is His life. This is our life. This life belongs to all Ruhnits. Tsiera, the darkness that is spreading is because some Ruhnits have changed throughout time. You know this more than others. The life of Wahid runs very deep in your blood, a gift from your mother. A time will come when many on Al-Ruh will change. Your skin is already showing the change. As Al-Wahid has told, this difference will cause strife amongst Ruhnits. Many will not relish the diversity. Darkness will continue to spread until Al-Wahid arrives. Tsiera, we are not alone on Al-Ruh. There are others here and even more on Abu and Ibn." Wahid's light had faded and the great arc of light Ruhnits called Darab Altibana stretched across the sky. "Tsiera, out within the great Darab Altibana, there are thousands more. Accept them abnataya alhabiba, accept them or die."

At that last word, the great Unark faded away. Tsiera gently shook Unark asking, "What do you mean more father? Father wake up, wake up." Tsiera knew, though, the life of Al-Wahid had left her father. Like the life force of Wahid on her hands earlier, she could feel Al-Wahid's gift had left her father. Tsiera carried her father to the stone outside and blazed forth her florescence calling on the life of Al-Ruh to take back the great Unark. "I will accept them, father, as I will accept Al-Wahid." As Tsiera turned to spread the word of his passing, the very essence of Unark was absorbed into the dirt of Al-Ruh.

Chapter 11

10:00 p.m. Tiradentes Day April 21, 2025

Jake and the crew had said their goodbyes to friends and family they would only communicate with virtually in the future and eventually not at all. They gave a special goodbye to the owner of the Ribeirinhos Club where they had spent time enjoying the last rays of sunshine on Earth swimming and enjoying each other's company. The local residents of Alcântara had really been celebrating Tiradentes Day for the last week, but today the festivities culminated into a special celebration of light ending with the requisite fireworks for any celebration. Only today, without their knowledge, they would be treated to a special, extra rocket in the sky.

It was not lost on the crew that only days ago they were learning about the Lady of Victory being called upon to save the Portuguese from the French. Now they were watching from their launch pad video feed, celebrations of the Brazil's past rebellion against the Portuguese to take back their country. The very ground they were launching from was rightfully owned by the slaves that were used to build Brazil. Yet again, they were to be displaced, run out and run over so Brazil and the US could launch more rockets from their land. Colonialism had wrecked havoc upon a world driven by greed for riches and the misplaced belief that being a Christian raised one above another, that being white made one better than a black, or a black better than a brown, or on and on and on. Father Joe had been thinking hard about this conundrum of the history of the world. Where had they so misconstrued the words and teachings and laws of God? Why had they so hated one another to take lives without concern? *My God my God why have you forsaken me,* the words of Jesus ran through his head. God did not forsake us; we have forsaken him and the true reckoning will begin.

They were timing the launch of the Falcon 9 carrying the Crew Dragon to coincide with the grand finale of the fireworks. Luckily through Pope Vieira's connections, they were on schedule to launch in 20 minutes. Every connoisseur of fireworks knew you had to have a grand finale after true darkness for the full effect of the show. Jake had asked Father Joe to say a few words before they launched. Father Joe had protested, but knew his task as crew counselor was now beginning, thus his ponderings about life and death and how things had gone so terribly wrong on Earth. "Jake asked me to say a few words tonight. As we have 10 minutes before we need to be fully strapped in, before our gloves and helmets are locked, let's gather together hand in hand. Look closely at the hand in your hand. Observe the lines in each palm. Feel the heat of the hand in your hand. Forget all the teachings of your youth, my friends, as they were fraught with error. Look at that hand in your hand and feel the heat of that hand in your hand. Let go of your faith beat into you from birth. Forget the Bible, the Koran, the Tripitaka, and all the other books and feel the heat of that hand in your hand. Feel the true power of creation. The life that flows through that hand is the same as the life that flows through your hand. We are one in the same. We are one in the same. White, black, brown, olive, heck, do we really need colors? God made us all one in the same. Where we go there can be nothing but unity. Kami no ibuki....the breath of God."

In true unity, hand in hand, all the races of the Earth combined together stating, "Kami no ibuki....the breath of God."

Strapped in and ready to go as the countdown reached 1, Abornazine Jones, member of the Abenaki Indian tribe, nuclear engineer and keeper of the light yelled out "Chegesawaa!!!! I make fire." And they made fire and the Falcon 9 launched the crew of NUERA1 into low earth orbit.

10:00 p.m. April 22nd

Low Earth Orbit - 30 minutes from docking with NUERA1

On command from *The Cross,* NUERA1's AI supercomputer was given the command to awake. *Magdalene* had been awake for months previously activating the environmental control and life support system, and growing Andreia's *Garden of Eden.* Put to sleep to save energy, she had laid ready to activate all major systems to prepare for docking of the crew. Happy to be awake to make ready for her occupants, *Magdalene* activated the full systems of life support, botany, navigation, and the command, communication, control center. No one could mistake the Vatican's programmers for not having a sense of humor.

Choosing the name of Mary Magdalene for NUERA1's super computer was both a devotion to the Cross and a suggestion of some rebellious nature. Only the chief programmer knew the full mission of the AI. The rest were simply given a task to code knowing that a parent program would control their subprograms. Sister Lisa, the most devoted follower of Pope Vieira amongst the Vatican's programmers, alone, knew the gravity of the true mission. She thought what more appropriate for the name than the most devoted follower of Jesus. She also thought that the crew could use a mother figure looking out for them. Magdalene looked out across the darkness of her orbit and thought *I see them*.

10:15 p.m. 15 minutes before docking

The crew of NUERA1 could barely see their final destination as the sun's rays illuminated only the few solar panels of the individual modules. Borrowing an idea from SpaceX, Pandere had coated each of the modules to reduce the albedo of the orbiting platform to near zero. SpaceX had received numerous complaints from the astronomical community about the brightness of their Starlink satellites. Pandere was not trying to appease astronomers, but instead make it difficult over time for anyone to track NUERA1. Of course, she had signal lights to avoid any unwanted collisions in their current orbit. Pandere was also fluctuating the inflation of the modules caused a wrinkling affect in the outer surface that would confuse radar.

10:25 p.m. 5 minutes before docking

"Oh meu Deus," Andreia softly spoke as their final home became visible through the view window. The rest of the crew did not need to understand Portuguese to glean the meaning behind those words. Several, out of habit, signed the cross. Abor, more than anyone, could appreciate the mass of NUERA1. He had worked the calculations numerous times designing the thorium drive that would thrust NUERA1 through space. Even he was speechless as he looked upon the most massive spacecraft by volume ever constructed. She was a spectacular site indeed. From their perspective, she continued to increase in size as they approached. Sitting out there in front of them was more than five times the usable volume of the International Space Station.

Jake had to fight to keep control at the view window as each one of NUERA1's crew gawked at the station. "Ok, enough sightseeing folks, buckle in, and let's get on board. Dragon to Vatican Control, we are proceeding with docking." Jake called it in, but they all knew the docking was autonomous. The Vatican was well aware they were closing in on the hatch.

Jake smiled to himself as he took in the view one last time before buckling himself in. This is NUERA1, our final resting place. As he took in the view one last time, he noticed the ever so slight reflectance of the sun off the inflated modules. It was fitting. The black expanded modules all strung together resembled the dark black rosary of his mother's as it would rest in a pile on her dresser. She was only missing the cross. Something he had broken off as a child. My final command....an interstellar rocket ship...on a mission for God. The butterflies had been growing in Jake's stomach for the last hour and he could sense the same from his crew. They were all excited to be beginning this mission but extremely nervous about the dangers they would face pulling this off. They all knew at some point their drive and unusual orbit would be noticed.

Chapter 12

8:00 a.m. May 31st

Feast of the Visitation of the Blessed Virgin Mary

Pope Vieira was saying mass for the Immaculate Blessed Virgin Mary. He had completed the ritual so many times in the past, but today was extra special. For he knew as he read the very words of Luke's gospel a new hope would be born again. "My soul doth magnify the Lord, and my spirit hath rejoiced in God my Savior. Because He that is mighty, hath done great things to me, and holy is His name," as Pope Vieira read those words, he felt an elation like no other. At that exact moment, the thorium drive of NUERA1 was activated. As his Holiness retired to his chambers later that morning, he could only hope that perhaps this time they would get it right. With a passing thought, he remembered Monsignor Mickey had not attended mass that day. Perhaps the invitation was late arriving.

8:00 a.m. NUERA1

"This is no drill. I repeat this is no drill. Batten the hatches, man your battle stations, dive, dive, dive," Hayat yelled out over the intercom to the crew making preparations for drive initiation. Jake gave Hayat a very stern look which faded slightly as he could see his drills had paid off. He could see on the monitors the entire crew was buckled in with helmets on in record time. Each was located in their key areas across the ship. Hayat quickly regained his composure, "Sorry Commander, it is just; I've always wanted to say that." The crew had been practicing safety drills until they were drilling in their sleep. What little sleep they could catch here and there, Jake had drilled them daily for the past month sharpening their skills like Archangel Michael's sword. They had dramatically reduced their time putting out the fake fires. The quick death of a spaceship, a fire, was the worst fear of any astronaut.

Jake had watched Hayat closely over the past few weeks. His expertise might be environmental controls, but his past military training was shining through. He had earned Jake's respect for his training and on a personal level Jake was beginning to like the man. "Hayat, there is something I have been meaning to discuss with you; with your love for submarines and all."

"Commander Young, I meant no offense really, Sir"

Jake laughed, "Hayat, being a fly boy, I take no offense. Heck, I grew up watching the same movies without the subtitles of course. Hayat, we are developing our chain of command on the fly with this mission. His Holiness wanted me to get to know the crew before choosing a second in command. I've seen the crew follow your lead without question during these drills. In case I ever become incapacitated, we need a second in command. How about being my XO?"

"Yes Sir," Hayat saluted with pride. "Sir, a Catholic and a Muslim ruling together, oh if my *Eimmy* could see us now."

"Yes indeed XO, now for you first order, you have got to straighten out Father Joe with his directions. Being a true man of the cloth, he did not watch all of our war movies as a kid; too much violence. The poor man is struggling deeply with port, starboard, fore, and aft."

"Drive control to the Comm.," Abor squawked over the radio. He was a bit nervous with all the hydrogen beginning to expel out the aft. Abor knew that the thorium- 228 drive was super heated at close to 3600K approaching nearly half the surface temperature of the Sun. If there were any errors in his design, they would know in 5 seconds. "Drive initiation in 5, 4, 3, 2, 1."

The drive began expelling hydrogen at 10 km/s. Not quite the kick in the pants afterburner thrust Jake remembered from his old Raptor. The drive thrust was a gentle push that would conserve fuel. It provided the needed constant thrust over time to spiral NUERA1 out of the Earth system to meet up with the Nautilus units at Lagrange point L1.

8:30 a.m.

Camp David, Maryland

President Buchanan rolled off of Laura as his private burn phone was ringing incessantly on his nightstand. "My God, Roger, do you realize what time it is?" Kurt was not in a good mood being disturbed from his visit with Laura. As his schedule demanded, it was getting more difficult to arrange a rendezvous. Luckily the first lady was out of the picture for the moment visiting her family on the west coast. He was able to arrange a special cocktail for Laura to make her *friendlier*. Her friends were trying to help her find God as she was becoming more resistant.

"Sir, my apologies, but you stated to alert you if anything unexpected developed." Roger was extremely nervous about alerting Kurt about this latest development. He had a really bad feeling about this Catholic retreat now in space.

"Yes, yes, Roger, get on with it!"

"Mr. President we have detected some unusual radiation readings coming from the NUERA1 retreat center. We had expected to see the normal LOX propulsion being used to obtain their residence orbit. However, I am told there is a thorium signature present in their drive system."

"Roger, my man, thorium is of no concern....they cannot weaponize it, so why worry?"

"Kurt you have never even bothered to read the reports, have you? Thorium can be used safely in reactors and for long duration rocket drives. Sir, coupled with the fact that they are not in a Hohmann transfer orbit but a spiral transfer orbit, we think they are not headed for a permanent Earth orbit as filed with the FCC."

The President, furious about being disturbed from his sexual play with Laura, was about to explode with this latest play of Antonio's. "God damn it Roger, why am I just now learning about this? And where now do we expect Antonio's retreat to be headed?"

Roger paused as he was beginning to detect things in his old friend that were disturbing. He was also afraid any further infractions might bring his time to an end on this Earth. Looking back, he was afraid his judgment would be swift and as he thought briefly, probably justified. "Mr. President, it now appears NUERA1's slow spiral orbital trajectory, if continued, will pass through the Lagrange point L1."

"Roger, if you want any chance of serving me further, you will get the precise coordinates of their orbital path to our friends in the alliance at Vandenberg Air Force Base. And Roger, do it now!"

President Buchanan hung up the phone and immediately called another private number of the residence of a general in the US Space Force sympathetic to the cause. "General, within the hour you will receive coordinates of a target we need to track and if necessary eliminate! Launch the X-37B as soon as you receive the information. General, I do not need to remind you that I never made this call!" Kurt's blood vessels were bulging in his neck as the darkness was coursing through his veins. Antonio's tiny little Vatican was beginning to be his largest thorn. Things were coming to a tipping point. The right wing evangelical world was at a point of taking over and dominating the

Christian world. This move by Antonio could play on the sympathies of many with his attempt to unite all humanity under the auspices of a God for all religions and races. Uniting all religions was a power play he could not allow as God was for the evangelical white man. Kurt knew if this happened he would lose support and power. This could not be allowed. The time had come for him to achieve total control. Picking up the phone Kurt placed one more call, "Steve, the time is upon us. Take care of Father Clanton as well. Make sure he has completed his mission first." Kurt hung up and left the bed leaving Laura behind. Something was nagging him about this Lagrange point L1 destination. What could that possibly achieve for the retreat, constant access to the Sun perhaps? As Kurt left the bedroom pondering the possibilities, Laura stayed as motionless as possible continuing to steady her breathing as if asleep.

Chapter 13

8:00 p.m. June 6th, In the Year of Our Lord 2025
Vatican City

His Holiness had not often visited the special vault where the Cross was operating. When his mission had begun, they had added the control center for the NUERA1 operation next to the Cross. The young operators in the control room were handpicked only by Pope Vieira. As Pope Vieira entered the room, some began to stand and bow or kneel before him. Quickly admonishing them for ignoring their stations, "NO, maintain your stations! Beloved followers of Christ, I am but a man. God's mission is of far more importance. We must pull this off without a hitch as those Yankees in America say."

"Your Holiness, all Crew Dragons with the remaining family members of the crew and the NUERA1 passengers have launched and are enroute to dock with NUERA1. The Cross has control and all craft will dock autonomously with NUERA1 with plenty of time before she reaches Lagrange point L1. There was some interference in our communications with the spaceport in Kourou, French Guiana. We believe once again the South Atlantic Anomaly is to blame. It appears one of our selected passengers suffered an unexplained heart attack at the last moment before the Crew Dragon was loaded. The communication was garbled, but the replacement as planned was ready and boarded. We just lost contact at the moment of launch before we got the name. Commander Young will have to sort it out in orbit."

9:00 p.m. June 7th

NUERA1

"Commander Young, we are tracking fifteen spacecraft inbound towards NUERA1." Mary alerted CCC from her navigation station. She had been manning the navigation unit, triple checking that their trajectory was indeed headed to Lagrange point L1. Though she knew the Cross was bringing up the Crew Dragons it never hurts to keep an eye on things. Mary did not fully trust AIs. Though she was enjoying some back and forth conversations with Magdalene, Mag, as she liked to call her on board NUERA1, she still hesitated in trusting her fully.

"Mary, I have confirmed with the Cross, this last craft is not a Crew Dragon. We have tracked its launch from your Vandenberg Air Force base." *Mag,* as Mary was now calling her, hesitated in alerting Mary of the origin. Learning how to interact with these humans, what information to reveal, and what to hold back, was part of her learning program. Her ultimate responsibility was the safety of the mission. She must make sure these humans did not change course.

"Commander Young, Mag, I mean Magdalene has confirmed, we have a bogey inbound."

"Understood Mary, we are tracking now." Jake had a feeling when he woke up this evening this was not going to be easy. Nothing was ever this easy. Up until now, there were just too many things going smoothly. Old man Murphy must have awakened. "XO prepare the crew as we may have to make a sudden course change. Magdalene, how much time do we have before the bogey is near our KOS?"

Magdalene had already calculated the Keep Out Sphere and knew the exact timing of the incoming Crew Dragons and the bogey. "Commander Young, the bogey will arrive within one hour of the last dragon docking.....also Commander, we have visual confirmation now, the bogey inbound is an X-37B."

Damn, Jake thought, one hour is outside the safety protocol for docking and egress of the Crew Dragons. Each Crew Dragon typically needed almost 3 hours to equalize pressure. Hayat, already reading Jake's mind was placing the call over the intercom, "Dr. Yoshioka, you are needed in CCC." Aiko arrived in short order. Just a few moments earlier, Magdalene had contacted her, alerting her that her presence might be needed in CCC.

Looking up, surprised to see Aiko so soon, "Thanks for the quick response, Dr."

"No problem Sir, Mag, I mean Magdalene gave me an alert".

Jake could appreciate the AIs programming thinking along the same lines as his. It was uncanny and a bit troubling that Magdalene would have sent an alert. He would have to discuss command protocols with Mag. Gee, now I am thinking it as well. Out of respect for her namesake, Mary Magdalene, he thought they should call her Magdalene. Mag was catchy though. "Dr. Yoshioka, we have a bogey inbound. I do not know its intent yet, but if it approaches our KOS before we have everyone on board we might have some decompression issues to deal with. Please be ready with medical protocols in place. Father Joe will assist you as well." Just as he spoke the name of Joe, Father Joe entered CCC. "Let me guess, Magdalene alerted you as well?" Father Joe shook his head yes. "Ok, Dr. Yoshioka and Dr. Washington, you are responsible for Crew Dragon egress. Assist the passengers with getting on board after pressurization. Our main concern is the Crew Dragon arriving from Kourou. They will not have time for full pressure equalization if this bogey has ill intents.

"Understood, Sir," Aiko and Joe left CCC together to work on arrival plans.

Yelling back at Aiko and Joe, "We have three hours, people."

Hayat approached Jake, "What is your thought, sir? I'm thinking these X-37Bs are unmanned and some new recruit at US Space Force command is at the controls on the ground."

"Hayat, exactly my thought. Let us hope that this young recruit forgets the laws of physics in orbit around a planet." Hayat with a very puzzled look on his face asked, "Sir?" Jake laughed as he knew Hayat's expertise was the environmental control system. Slapping the XO on the back,"Where were you when NASA first tried docking two spacecraft in space, Hayat?"

12:00 Midnight

NUERA1

"Medical to CCC, we have thirteen of the Crew Dragons egressed and passengers are settling in. The last Crew Dragon has begun pressure equalization."

Aiko sent her report to CCC as Mark Leo, Abor's son was the last of the first group of passengers to get on board. His eyes were as big as saucers as he took in the craft. He held tightly to the waste bag, as he was very queasy from the effects of zero gravity.

"Understood, Aiko, keep all passengers strapped in until further notice," Jake called from CCC right as Mag announced over the intercom "KOS alert, I repeat KOS alert."

12:00 Midnight Eastern Standard Time
The United States of America

Across the United States, members of the America Alliance were initiating PIERCE, Patriot Immigrant Eradication and Revolution of Christian Evangelicals for America. Starting on the east coast, the first device blew in New York, and then Miami. Roger had just arrived at his hotel in Jakeson, Florida after making arrangements in Kourou. He was going to observe and report the results in Miami to President Buchanan. As he entered his hotel room and reached for the light, a bullet entered his skull as a Patriot silenced Father Roger Clanton for good. The Alliance working their way west activated the devices in Atlanta, then Chicago, New Orleans, and Houston. Finally reaching the west coast, the last three devices were activated in Los Angeles, San Francisco, and Seattle. Steve placed the call to Kurt Buchanan before the first media report hit the air waves letting him know it was done.

1:00 a.m.

Oval Office, White House, Washington, D.C.

There was a purpose to the timing of the American Alliance's bombs. Catching many people at sleep in their homes increased the casualty rate two fold. The President could also use the lack of any coordinated response at this time of night from opposing parties to his next act. "My fellow Americans, it is with great sadness and trepidation that I announce the enactment of martial law. Nine of our major cities tonight are under siege. I have been informed that the terrorists used tactical nuclear weapons targeting some of the greatest cities of America." To avoid smiling, President Buchanan was stabbing his letter opener into his thigh. "The estimates at this time are we have lost close to a million Americans. My experts tell me we will lose another half a million from the radiation fallout. It is not understood at this time why these particular cities were targeted. There are those who are speculating that the devices were being transported by illegal immigrants and perhaps were detonated prematurely before setup in more established areas of our fine cities. Until further notice, there will be an 8:00 a.m. to 6:00

p.m. curfew across the land. Our borders are closed
indefinitely and there is no travel outside these United
States. I have called up all branches of the military to
secure our land. All National Guard units are now under
federal control. Patriot forces from across our great land
are being called up to assist with securing these cities
once the radiation has subsided. These fine men,
volunteers all, will go city to city securing them and
looking for survivors that may have found shelter. For
now we ask for your prayers for our great nation. May
God bless you and May God bless America!"

1:00 a.m.

NUERA1 Orbit

"KOS ALERT, KOS ALERT, BOGEY INBOUND,"
Magdalene repeated the warning again with more
emphasis.

Adding to the warning, Hayat, NUERA1's XO, jumped on the intercom, "All NUERA1 crew don your pressure suits. All passengers stay in your flight suits. Prepare for impact." Hayat was not exaggerating this time or playing back some Hollywood movie in his mind. This was real and real lives were at stake. Though, he was hoping that Commander Jake Young really had something up his sleeve, like they always did in Hollywood movies.

Jake pushing behind Hayat checking system readouts, "Mag, is the system ready?"

"Commander, the system is ready. I warn, though, you will leave only a portion left for maneuvers like this later."

Jake knew the chance he was taking. What was the point of having high thrust later if they all died now? Aiko and Father Joe has been talking the last Crew Dragon through the pressure procedures. They were also trying to calm the passengers down. Losing a member of their manifest to the heart attack and taking on a new member had them frazzled from launch. "CCC to dock 14, open the hatch and bring them on board. Upon my mark, prepare for emergency decompression." Jake called it in hoping and praying Aiko and Father Joe were prepared.

1:05 a.m.

Vandenberg Air Force Base X-37B Control Room

First Lieutenant Johnny Cole had received the orders to destroy the station. They came straight from the top they said and he could not ignore a direct order. He had only just graduated from simulation training before this mission. The last Lieutenant had been removed from command after the accident in Brazil. He did not want to repeat the same mistakes and was jumping to show he had the right stuff. He could see the station on his monitor straight in front of him. Knowing he was already in the Keep Out Sphere area he knew they had to be aware of his presence. NUERA1 was within three thousand feet and straight in front of his X-37B. He could not wait any longer and punched the max thrust button on his console waiting to see the destruction on his monitor.

1:05:30 a.m.

NUERA1 Orbit

"Rocket flare visible, Rocket flare visible," Magdalene yelled adding volume to the message to CCC for emphasis.

The hairs raised on the back of Jake's neck. He had been in this situation before over Syria. He could feel the imminent danger but then he was not fast enough to avoid the missile. He knew he would only get this chance once as the operator of the X-37B would quickly learn their mistake. "30 Seconds Magdalene and then initiate max delta V and blow the hatch on dock 14."

"Counting down, Commander."

Thirty seconds seemed like an eternity to Jake. It was not just his life at stake this time. All toll, there were about 100 passengers and crew aboard NUERA1. If they did not pull this off..... Magdalene had run the numbers only once confident in her program. Counting down three, two, one, she initiated the max delta V just as the Sun's rays broke the horizon. Simultaneously, she blew the hatch on dock 14 decompressing the air lock. Jake had banked on there being just enough pressure difference to blow off the Crew Dragon. The NUERA1 felt a jolt throughout the spacecraft and hard g-force to port and then silence.

1:10 a.m.

Vandenberg Air Force Base X-37B Control Room

Thinking the NUERA1 had exploded and flooded his sensors, First Lieutenant Johnny Cole jumped for joy. In reality his front camera of his X-37B recorded the flash of sun rays off the white heat shield of the Crew Dragon before it impacted the X-37B. It would be hours later when he learned his rookie mistake. Something NASA had learned very early in spaceflight.

2:00 a.m.

NUERA1

Vatican Control had relayed the news to the crew about the events in the United States. They were professional and they had a mission. They were also human and felt extreme guilt for what they were leaving behind; a world spiraling out of control and a world where darkness was spreading. Aiko and Father Joe kept themselves busy administering 100% oxygen to the last Crew Dragon passengers. They had created a temporary hyperbaric chamber using another air lock to aid with the decompression sickness. Aiko supplemented this with shots of nonsteroidal anti-inflammatory drugs (NSAIDs) and corticosteroids to help reduce swelling in their joints and tissues. Luckily, the capsule that was jettisoned was not far from equalization when they had to egress. It served its purpose as the X-37B rammed into it as the rest of NUERA1 increased velocity to move to a higher orbit. Abor reconnected with his family, giving Mark Leo a big hug and took them on a private tour of the facility. As a distraction, Mary went down to the Garden of Eden as Andreia called it to assist with gathering food for the meals being planned for the passengers. Jake and his XO remained in CCC monitoring their systems to rendezvous with the Nautilus. The passengers had not yet been informed.

Hayat assisting Jake with the upcoming presentation to the passengers could not resist, "Commander how did you know? I mean, was that not a big risk?"

Jake considering his words carefully, "Yes, it was a risk. A risk we had to take as there were no other options. Plus, I had faith, Hayat. I prayed the pilot of the X-37B would make the same mistake made by NASA years ago. I banked on the fact that the US Space Force is new and in the rush to get young lieutenants trained perhaps one or two would forget. Your intuition tells you can just go in a straight line in space. In reality, you are free falling around the Earth. I had faith the person manning that X-37B would forget Kepler's third law. We were ahead in orbit and he just punched the thrust. All he did was increase his altitude away from NUERA1, and in the process increased his orbital period. Poor guy moved himself above and behind us."

"Commander, why blow the hatch then for the Crew Dragon?"

"Buying us time, XO, buying us time. If I am right, for a time, until the radar folks flag him down with new scans, he will think he blew us up when the Sun flashed off the Crew Dragon just before his X-37B impacted it."

"Alhamdulillah!"

"Yes, praise be to God indeed. Ok, I had better inform the passengers."

"There was a time, my friends, I had the faith of a child. I never questioned God or my path in His realm. I know many of you probably thought as I did and then you got older. We thought the covenant we took before Saint Peter's tomb was some trick of light. A cheap story worst case and perhaps a free ride into space at best. Mark my words as I have seen many things recently that have bolstered my faith. I will tell you it was neither a cheap light show, nor a free trip. Except for the very young amongst us, we will pay for this trip with our lives. Our children will carry forward and bring His word to another civilization. As I'm told now it has happened this way for millennia. Below us on Earth, the reckoning has begun. There will be great darkness before the balance of light wins over. As I speak to you now, we have seen a great loss of life in the United States. Nine cities have been all but destroyed with tactical nuclear weapons. Martial law has been declared and the rights of many have now been vanquished. The darkness is spreading across the world with other countries seeing similar destruction of cities. Similiar devices with different yields have denotated in Budapest, Vienna, Zurich, Jerusalem, Moscow, Beijing, and more. Yahwehians who refuse to follow His light, those cast out of heaven long ago, are raining terror upon the Earth. Know this my friends, the reckoning has begun and darkness will not win. There is one upon the Earth who will bring back the light."

As Jake finished, he could feel the tension on NUERA1. The silence after the last of his words emanated from the intercom could be felt as if a lead blanket had been laid upon them. As his words settled upon the passengers only the quiet hiss of the environmental control system could be heard. It was Magdalene who broke the silence. The AI had been aboard NUERA1 in total silence for so long she could not handle the quiet any longer. She had begun to appreciate these humanoids aboard. Ever so quietly she began playing the notes of *Oh God Beyond All Praising* across the ship. Taking from his Planet's Jupiter melody, Gustav Holst had created the hymn to praise God. For Magdalene it served not only to praise God but to raise the spirits of those she had taken on board.

9:00 p.m. Sunday June 15th

St Ann's Catholic Church, Washington, D.C.

Laura waited until the last of the Sunday church service had left and caught the door before it closed. With the curfew in place, only the sisters from the local convent were allowed to attend in person. The rest of the parish had to attend virtually. Laura had a special letter from the President that gave her the ability to come and go as she pleased for special visits to the White House. No Patriot would stop her after curfew. She could see the priest and the acolytes were finishing up blowing out candles and locking up the Eucharist. As their backs were turned, she quickly snuck into the confessional at the back of the church. As she knelt, she made a silent prayer to God that they would leave before discovering her. At times she would shake uncontrollably as her system fought the drugs President Buchanan had been pumping into her. The clinic had been giving her Lofexidine tablets. As she fumbled with her purse to find the last tablet, one of the acolytes came to the confessional to do a final check before locking up. Laura held her breath as beads of sweat dripped down her forehead, praying again to God to conceal her presence. The young acolyte, more interested in something on her phone than performing her duties, quickly passed by the confessional and turned the deadbolt on the front door of the church. Laura heard the priest and acolytes leaving out the back as she left the confessional dry swallowing her last Lofexidine tablet.

Laura moved over to the votive candle rack kneeling to pray as she lit a candle. As she prayed, calm came over her and the shakes subsided. She was too deep in prayer to realize that the calm was not from the tablet, as it typically took her several hours to feel any effect from those. His Holy Spirit continued to spread across Laura as she prayed. Ever so softly Laura continued to whisper her prayers to God, "Heavenly Father, I ask you to forgive my cousin, Katrina, for her indiscretions oh Lord. Please allow her into heaven to serve You Father. Our life in Hazard, KY was not an easy one, Father. Katrina and I both just wanted a different life; to get out of Hazard and away from him. I know Katrina stopped praying, Lord. She was lost trying to protect me. God, I still do not understand why You would allow it. Why would You let him hurt us? I prayed and prayed and still he hurt us. A man...a man of the cloth, God. He would come home from seminary and You let him hurt us? Why God, please tell me why You would let Uncle Mike hurt us?" Laura began to sob and cry quietly with her eyes closed. She could not see the light beginning to grow around her. "We told our priest Father but he ignored our pleas. Summer after summer he would hurt us and yet, You did nothing. Katrina was damaged, Father. Damaged beyond the physical bruises; she was lost to him, Father. Her very soul was crying and begging for help and yet, still You did not stop him!! Why God? Why?" Overcome by grief for the loss of her cousin, Laura caught herself realizing this was not why she came here today, to blame God. Squeezing her eyes even tighter and clenching her enclosed hands together, Laura began praying with all her might. "Forgive me Father, I know not Your reasons for I am but a simple woman. I did not come here to blame You. I came here to ask forgiveness for Katrina and beg you to save her soul. Allow Saint Peter to open the very gates of Heaven wide to receive her, Father. Please God hear me! Hear me! Hear me!"

Blinding light burst forth from the Votive candles as he made known his presence. "Open your eyes, child of God! Open your eyes!" Laura Flaherty opened her eyes, wiping away the tears so she could see clearly as she thought her mind was playing tricks on her. Standing before her was the most beautiful sight she had ever seen. The creature had the features of a man, but the wings stretched out behind him filled the room. "Laura your cousin stands next to Him in Heaven now. There was never anything to forgive as you and Katrina have been servants of God from your birth. I cannot explain His ways but know He felt your pain. With each altercation, He felt your pain. Tears flowed from His eyes."

Laura could see the truth in the words spoken by this creature. As she took in the full visage before her, she could see the golden battle armor across his chest, arms, and legs. Full of many scars, she knew this was a warrior; a warrior for God. It could be none other than Archangel Michael. "Forgive me Archangel Michael, Forgive me!" Laura dropped to the floor spreading herself flat in homage to Archangel Michael.

"Rise Laura, do not give homage to me!" Archangel Michael quickly pulled Laura from the floor and sat her down. "It is I who should give homage to you for the suffering you have endured in His name. The darkness is spreading across this world, but with your help we will bring His light to balance again. We need your help Laura. Reaching down to the golden greave of his right leg, Archangel Michael pulled forth a small dagger. Placing it in Laura's hands, he spoke one word "Yahweh" and the dagger began to pulse with life subtly glowing.

"No Archangel Michael, He said *Thou Shall Not Kill*!"

"Yes Laura that is His command, but in this case he is already dead. Your President Buchanan gave his life to the darkness years ago. He must be stopped now before the darkness further spreads beyond our control. God commands it." As he spoke the last words, Archangel Michael turned and strode out of the church. Laura ran to the window to see the angel leave and caught a fleeting glimpse of Archangel Michael and an entire platoon of warriors for God vanish into the night.

10:00 p.m.

NUERA1 Orbit closing on Lagrange point L1

The melancholy mood aboard NUERA1 had gotten worse since the nine city disaster. Some unrest had been brewing amongst the passengers and the crowded quarters did not help. Word has reached NUERA1 of war breaking out across the Earth. Countries trying to come to the aid of the United States were being attacked by the Patriots forces serving President Buchanan. The Patriots serving the American Alliance had managed to infiltrate every branch of the military. Where they could not influence and encourage allegiance, they were out right killing soldiers under the false charge of treason. A group of passengers lead by a priest had tried to convince Jake to let them go back to the Earth. The priest, injured in the decompression accident, with his face still covered in bandages had managed to spread some discord. His talk of blasphemy amongst the Vatican's elite was disconcerting. Jake thought it was about time for the ship's counselor, Father Joe, to step into his role. That would have to wait as the immediate concern was docking with the Nautilus.

"Passenger and Crew of NUERA1, prepare for docking," Jake announced from CCC as passengers and his crew strapped in across the ship. The necessity of using the LOX tanks from the individual modules earlier to boost their orbit increased their speed to dangerous levels for docking. As Abor had informed him they could not at this point disengage the thorium drive. Their only alternative was to use the LOX tanks again with a delta V at just the right moment to slow the ship to dock without catastrophic results.

Abor had been working with *Magdalene* for the past 24 hours running simulation after simulation for a solution. They had lost contact with Vatican Control so they were on their own now. "Mag are you sure this is going to work? My numbers show we are dangerously close to docking mechanism failure." Abor had been awake for 24 hours straight stressing over his calculations. His speciality was nuclear propulsion not structural engineering. He was a little rusty on his Methods of Materials.

"Abor, all conditions will be nominal if not slightly over the max tolerance range."

"Mag, slightly over the max tolerance range and we are slightly dead."

"Abor, I have volumes of mechanical stress theorems in my database. The NUERA1 will dock safely. Remember all good engineers use a factor of safety."

"Factor of safety?!? You mean you are relying on some design engineer's factor of safety? What if they cut the factor of safety to save costs?"

Mag had gone over this thousand of times more than Abor in her internal AI brain, running all possible scenarios. Her program, though, had not considered this absence of a factor of safety. *To save costs* she thought over saving lives made no sense to her programming. It was not logical. She no longer had a connection with the Cross or she would have had him run the same simulations to confirm. Oddly her programming kept coming up with something that made no logical sense, but yet it was inside her. She confirmed multiple times, it was the root of her programming, faith. "Abor, we must have faith!"

10:30 p.m.

West Wing of the White House, Washington, D.C.

President Buchanan had already shoed away his staff. Only his Patriot squad of goons stood watch around the residence. The real heroes of the Secret Security Service had long been killed for insubordination and

thus treason to the high command. His plans of
domination were going well. The United States was
strictly locked down under his declaration of martial
law and most of the military was falling in line.
Without any proof to the contrary, they could only
believe that the nine cities disaster was truly a terrorist
attack. Little did they know it was then Senator
Buchanan who fought so gallantly for the 2007
National Defense Authorization Act. Buried deep inside
that 500+ page document was the clause giving the now
President Buchanan the very right to declare martial
law. Everything was going according to plan except
Antonio. Kurt's smug smile turned to a slight frown as
he thought about the reports from Steve. Steve had
taken care of the young lieutenant at Vandenberg Air
Force Base, but the damage had been done. They had
missed their chance again to stop Antonio. On his
screen was live coverage from the US Space Force
displaying the NUERA1 retreat center as it closed in on

the Lagrange point L1. Two blips on a screen slowly becoming one. For what, nobody seemed to know. There was nothing there except SOHO, the Solar and Heliospheric Observatory. SOHO had been placed there in a halo orbit about the Lagrange point L1 to monitor the sun. Was Antonio taking them on a field trip?

10:31 p.m.

NUERA1

"Commander Young, you need to look at this," Mary Harrington from navigation called to alert Jake. "There is nothing there except the SOHO observatory. I have had Mag repeat the radar scans multiple times and there is nothing there except SOHO. Mag continues to direct us on this course despite this fact.

Jake called out, "Mag...I mean Magdalene" thinking damn there goes all protocol in a tense situation "Please report coordinates of Nautilus gravity module Alpha Omega".

"Commander Young, Nautilus gravity module Alpha Omega is dead ahead, Sir."

"Magdalene, your own radar scans show there is nothing there but SOHO. Please confirm. We are 9 minutes from docking. We should have visual confirmation of Nautilus at this point and we are closing fast on SOHO. Please confirm."

"Commander Young, I have cross referenced all my programming and the last accurate location from the Cross shows the Nautilus is dead ahead."

10:35 p.m.

The White House

A slight knock on the door was all that alerted President Buchanan of his visitor. His grumpy demeanor evaporated as Laura entered wearing a body suit that left nothing to the imagination, slightly obscured only by a thin shaw. Laura seemed to be coming around to his way of thinking. She had accented her outfit with a new pair of bright red steel studded stiletto heels. Perhaps she was beginning to enjoy our little sessions. Laura walked cat like over to the desk pushing President Buchanan away in his chair and began unzipping his pants. Pulling up the very thin material of her body suit, she mounted President Buchanan in his chair and began to please him.

10:37 p.m

NUERA1

"Magdalene, run it again!" Jake was beside himself. He never would have believed he would be arguing with an AI about something that is obviously, per its own scans, not there.

"Commander Young, we have just reconnected with the Cross. I am receiving confirmation from someone at Vatican Control. The Nautilus is there."

I have one hundred souls depending on me, Jake thought. Perhaps the computers got the SOHO location confused somehow with the Nautilus. Perhaps the Nautilus never made it to the Lagrange point L1. Perhaps it was off course in the Lagrange Halo orbit and they could reacquire its position later. Too many variables, but he was not going to ignore what his own eyes showed him. "Magdalene, again your own radar scans show only the SOHO which we are going to collide with in 3 minutes. On my command, prepare an emergency abort sequence to initiate in 2 minutes. I want a hard to port maneuver on my mark."

10:39 p.m.

The White House

Laura's mouth had begun to fill with blood as she bit down hard on her tongue using pain to advert her attention from the act. As she rose up and down pleasing the President, the disgusting images of the man beneath her began to make her stomach revolt. President Buchanan had succumbed to the darkness completely and apparently no longer even gave a care about personal cleanliness. Thankfully, he cared not for kissing as his teeth had rotted and a foul stench resulted. His skin beneath all the makeup was oozing a grey greasy matter out of his pores. Laura, at the breaking point thinking she could no longer continue awoke to a sunny meadow. Across the meadow was her beautiful cousin Katrina running with her favorite Labrador, Buck. Katrina looked up and waved as the sun spread its rays across the meadow to reach Laura.

Katrina ran across the meadow with her dog, Buck, to meet up with Laura. Knocking her down in the tall grass, she smothered her with a bear hug as Buck licked her all over her face. As the warmth of the Sun's rays beamed down upon them, Laura was filled with love and joy and the power of the Holy Spirit. Katrina whispered in her ear, "Now." Laura reached down into the grass and picked up the stick that had been lying there and tossed it across the meadow for Buck to fetch.

10:40 p.m.

NUERA1

"Abort! Abort! Abort! Damn you Abort!" Jake was continuing to punch the emergency abort sequence to no avail.

"Jake, I have a message from the Cross," Magdalene softly called to CCC.

"I'm just a little busy at the moment, Mag!" Jake yelled back.

"Daddy, stop!" The voice he heard next could not possibly be real. It was the voice of little Jackie, his daughter. Impossible he thought, as she was dead. "Daddy, stop," the voice cried again and this time Jake stopped and turned away from the computer screen. Images of his life were flashing through his mind. The loss of his brother, his grandfather, his divorce, the accident, the hundreds of lives he had taken as a soldier; he was not going to make the wrong decision again. He was not going to lose these lives. *The pain, the fear, the shame...* "Daddy, stop, you have to have faith, Daddy."

Time froze as Jake looked up and out the view window of the CCC. At the very last moment, the SOHO spacecraft moved out of the way, missing NUERA1 by a cat's hair. The crew would always talk later that they swear they could feel the space between the craft compress as they passed. For a moment nothing happened and nothing was visible beyond the SOHO. Where were the blessed stars? Out there looking away from the Sun there should have been stars, but for a large portion of their view they could see nothing. The crew erupted in applause and Jake could only think *Bill Pandere, my friend, our savior, you did it!* Jake punched the intercom and alerted the passengers, "Final docking procedures initiated brace yourselves." NUERA1 closed the gap to contact the locking mechanism docking with Nautilus Alpha Omega with passengers sensing only a slight reaction force. The large artificial gravity structure of the Nautilus before them had a long docking bay and air lock aft, progressing forward to the propulsion and control center. Beyond you could see the large twin gravity modules for hundreds of yards. Forward of these was the largest observation deck every constructed, the grand cupula.

Looking out the window again, Jake suddenly realized what shape the Nautilus represented. It was the Holy Cross. Jake, watching his crew, Abor, Aiko, Andreia, Joe, Mary, and his friend, Hayat, before him all hugging and giving high fives. He could not help but to see them as apostles. Representatives from the very best of all the Earth's races making the ultimate sacrifice on the cross to carry His word to another world to save them from the darkness, their sins. His mom's rosary had been repaired as the cross had been reconnected to the beads of prayer. Jake had received the ultimate gift, faith. Not the Catholic faith, not the faith of some monstrous Christian Church sprawling across 3 city blocks, or the simple Baptist Church on a country corner. No, Jake had received the faith of the one true God, Yahweh, Allah, Wakan Tanka, Manitou, and known by so many other names. The faith of the Great Spirit without the four walls of a church was the greatest gift of all.

10:40 p.m.

The White House

The Patriots, guarding the door to the President's chambers, heard a loud noise that brought them out of their slumber. Receiving no response to their knocks on the door, they rushed into the room to investigate. President Buchanan was slumped over in his chair as if asleep. Sticking out the back of his neck was an ornate dagger of some considerable age buried to the hilt with the blade severing his brain stem. Laura lay dead before him on the desk covered head to toe in a very modest golden white dress. Analysis by the forensics team later would reveal the material was of some unknown origin. The lab tech had tried to include some nonsense about feathers. His superiors fired him immediately and destroyed his data. He could later be found lighting a candle daily at St Ann's Church for a Laura Flaherty, pausing often to give reverence to the painting of Archangel Michael.

Epilogue

August 1st, 2025

NUERA1 Solar System Transit Orbit

Jake looking out into the darkness of space, felt a little unnerved by the expanse before him. The grand cupola utilized a new material that was as strong as steel but crystal clear. If not for the hand holds in place, floating in zero gravity in here could frighten a few with height phobia, he thought. He preferred having the seat of his Raptor at his back when flying. He thought this was probably what it was like floating in his mother's womb until he got too big to move, of course. He came up to the GC as the passengers were calling it under the guise of a safety inspection. Before it was opened for use, it was a place he could be alone with his thoughts mulling over the events of the past few weeks.

One would have thought the millions of deaths and the spread of darkness on the Earth would have troubled him the most. Rather, it was the small quiet voice of his daughter echoing in his mind, "Daddy, you must have faith," that rocked his world. Earlier, as the gravity modules were spun up to speed to simulate the constant 1g gravity of Earth, the passengers of NUERA1 had waited like ants in a flood at the air lock. Pressing with excitement, they waited impatiently to spread out and find their living quarters after the cramped confines of their original containment. It was all Jake and the XO could do to keep some semblance of order. His daughter's voice nagging him in the back of his mind, he watched the passengers before him; almost one hundred souls of responsibility, every possible trade from plumbers to scientists. All races of the world present with every color, religion, creed and sex represented.

How would he keep order and sustain the same excitement evident before him for the mission of a lifetime? Sure, the Vatican had prepared a plan and they would follow it for a start. Jake knew from his combat experience, plans are only as good as the paper on which they are written. It was so cliche to think it, but you had to adapt and overcome. We must adapt and overcome. He worried that overcoming thousands of years of war, racism, hatred, almost genetically bred into them might be insurmountable. At its root, judgment. Humans had been passing judgment upon one another since Adam and Eve. Judging themselves more worthy than another, their physical stature, the color of their skin, their sex, their ideas, and their beliefs. There was his daughter's voice again, "You have to have faith, Daddy."

Faith had not worked on the Earth. The raging destruction across the world was proof of that. The reckoning was spreading, rampaging across the land. The Yahwehians, angel warriors for God, were fighting to bring back the light, the goodness in all, but at what cost? Reports reaching NUERA1 told of countless innocents lost. The blade of Archangel Michael was blackened with the darkness being expelled from the land. The Militia Sancti Petri's ranks were thinning losing thousands trying to defend the Vatican. They had pushed back the first dark wave, but not after his Holiness had succumbed to a heart attack. Jake's former commander had reported via a secure channel the death of President Buchanan. The vice president totally unprepared to lead had taken his own life. The Speaker of the House was calling for new elections to appease the masses while they tried to root Patriots out of command positions. Faith, how will I use faith to keep NUERA1 from splitting at the seams?

Aiko floated through from the Alpha gravity module joining Jake at his side. As if reading his thoughts, she placed her hand upon his shoulder. "Commander, Jake, I heard her voice." Father Joe, Andreia, Mary, Abor, and Hayat floated in behind her as she continued, "Jake, we all heard her voice. With faith we will follow you through the very gates of hell to fight for the light. Not with faith alone, Jake, with love. We will learn to love one another again. With faith and love our diversity will unite." Aiko's hand lingered a bit longer on Jake's shoulder squeezing ever so softly. As she turned to float back to the Medical Bay, "Oh, Commander, I almost forgot to report. The passenger who sustained the major injuries during the decompression is awake again. Sir, I have removed the facial bandages and Mag says even with the damage her facial recognition program can confirm. There are no records of this individual in our manifest."

Monsignor Mike Flaherty looked around the Medical Bay, confused, and delirious having been strapped in for his own protection. He kept mumbling under his breath, "Heretics, heretics, I will kill them all, Antonio's alien chariots of fire, blasphemy, generation ship, blasphemy, I will serve you, Lord."

20 light-years away, destination Gliese 667C (c) - also known by Ruhnits as Al-Ruh:

Tsiera saddened with grief for the loss of her father, the great Unark, went on a Rihlat Al'iiman to renew the teachings of her father within. Following the path of Darab Altibana through the sky where it reached the horizon, her journey of faith continued for days. Days turned into weeks, weeks into months, and months into years. Tsiera traveled her Rihlat Al-iiman meeting the many different inhabitants of Al-Ruh her father had mentioned. She found many strange Ruhnits across the land. Everywhere she professed the coming of Al-Wahid. Many of the Qadim with their life force waning would not listen. The Saghira would welcome her with open arms and open minds. Their youthful minds knew not of judgment. They knew not of hate. They cared not she glowed blue from the essence of Al-Ruh. Listening to and heeding the stories of the great Unark, they prepared for the coming of Al-Wahid. They prepared for the coming of God.

Arabic Translations

Abi: My father

Abnataya Alhabiba: My beloved daughter

Abu: Father

AL- : The

Alayhi al-salam: Peace be upon him

Aldamu: The blood

Alhamdulillah: Praise be to God

Alhaya: Life

Al-Ruh: The spirit

Alsalam ealaykum: Peace be upon you

Al-Wahid: The one

Damu: Blood

Dhilal: Shadows

Ibn: Son

Ithnaan: Two

Khitaya: Sins

Khitayana: Our sins

Khutba: Sermon

Mikhaeel: Michael

Mudamir Alshari: Destroyer of Evil

Qadim: Old

Rihlat Al'iiman: Trip of Faith

Ruh: Spirit

Saghira: Young

Thalaatha: Three

Thoqob 'aswad: Black Hole

Yad Allah ealayk: May the hand of God be upon you

Zalazil: Quakes

<u>Upcoming Release</u>

I had great fun writing this novel about NUERA1. I hope you enjoyed the book and perhaps have a different point of view on religion and space travel. If you enjoyed the book please leave a review at www.amazon.com.

The GENSHIP trilogy continues with book two in the year of our Lord 2022.